CHAPTER 1

"Hey, cowboy, where are you heading?"

Jake Stewart had been stretching his back while watching an attendant pump gas into his RV at a truck stop a little south of Portland — Oregon was still one of those states that didn't allow motorists to pump their gas — when a woman on the other side of the island asked about his destination.

She was a little shorter than his five-ten, with red hair spilling out of a sports cap, a black studded leather jacket, jeans, and a white shirt with a snap front. Not all the snaps were snapped.

"I'm going to the Washington coast. How about yourself?" He guessed she was from one of the other RVs, semi-trucks, cars with families on vacation, or service vans crowding the truck stop. She didn't look like a working woman trolling for business.

"The Washington coast sounds great. Want a passenger?"

Before Jake could stumble out an answer, the gas hose handle clicked off. Jake looked down to see a burp of gas spit out from the RV. Damn, 65 gallons, the gauge read — over $300 — good for about 300 miles. These older RVs were cheap to buy but serious gas hogs.

"Sure," he said, getting his credit card back from the attendant. "The other side is unlocked. Hop in."

This was day two of Jake's 1,300-mile drive from Arizona to Washington on what could be termed a mission of mercy, and maybe a passenger was just what he needed to keep him alert. Especially a passenger as good-looking as this one.

Jake opened the driver's door, tossed his canvas Australian slouch hat with the brim of one side dashingly pinned up — which he had purchased on a lark to keep the desert sun off his head and would likely qualify for a cowboy hat Down Under — onto the cowl covering the engine between the seats and watched his new passenger scramble into the elevated cab.

When she bent over to grab the edge of the seat to pull herself up, Jake caught a fleeting glimpse down her shirt.

Good god, thought Jake, grow up, man. Still, he felt a spring in his weary body when he grabbed the steering wheel to pull himself up.

"We should hurry a little," she said, fastening her seat belt. "Time and tide wait for no man."

The RV's engine roared to life — there's a gallon gone, Jake thought as he shifted into gear and, seeing a break in traffic, accelerated for the opening.

Bang, bang, bang!

"Damn it, what did I hit?" Jake let up on the gas halfway out into traffic, looking into the passenger-side mirror to see an angry man banging his flat palm on the rig.

"Jessie, you come back here, you bitch! I'll get you; I'll get you!"

BWAAAAH, a truck's air horn blasted to Jake's left. Jake whipped his head around to see a pissed-off driver in a semi, smoke rolling from its braking tires. No time to hesitate now. Jake's foot smashed down the gas pedal, and the hunkering rig finished the turn into traffic.

"Who was that? What was that all about? Should I turn around?" A glance into the mirror showed the angry man reaching into a coat pocket — for a gun? Instead, the man whipped out a phone to take photos of the receding RV.

"I don't know, nothing to do with me," said his passenger. She tilted down the visor and looked at herself in the vanity mirror.

She was pretty, freckles dotting her cute nose and high cheekbones. Lines around her lips and eyes gave her age at 35 plus, like Jake, which made Jake comfortable. Women in their early 20s made him nervous.

"He seemed to know your name. Jessie, was it?"

"Yeah, that's not me. My name is... Ruby. Like my hair." She took off the cap and shook out her hair. Definitely red. Natural or dyed, still heart-stopping red.

Tilting his head towards a knitted shoulder bag she had placed on the cowl, he asked, "Would you like me to drop you somewhere or take you to get your belongings?"

What had he gotten himself into? He didn't want to drive the 32-foot motorhome towing his Toyota Tacoma pickup all over Portland on errands for Ruby/Jessie. He definitely didn't want to reencounter the angry man.

"I'm good. No stops. Just drive on. Don't let me hold you back." She pulled a small brush from her bag to run through her hair.

A long, low rumble followed by a sudden loud crack jerked Jake's attention to the sky. Dark clouds threatening heavy rain all day opened, and the deluge began.

Great, thought Jake, just as I'm crossing over the Columbia River into Washington. The I-5 bridge, with its narrow lanes and tight sides hemming in big vehicles like the RV, should have been replaced 20 years ago. It was all Jake could do to contain the loose-steering RV to his lane as rain pelted the windshield and big trucks sprayed up blinding waves of oily water.

"Why doesn't my side have a wiper?"

"I bought this rig in Arizona from a guy who said he was too old to drive it anymore. While it's more than 35 years old, he swore he always kept it in perfect condition. I hadn't driven it a mile before the wiper there fell off. In Arizona, keeping the rain off the windshield is not a big issue."

Once across the bridge, the freeway shoulders widen out. The big '80s V-10 Ford engine purred along — burning up a gallon of gas every four to five miles — and the one wiper did just enough for Jake to see the road.

At Longview, 50 miles north of Portland, Jake exited I-5 to turn left towards the coast.

Tomorrow was Monday; he hoped to be at his new job by then. He still had another 70 miles on curvy roads, and this rain was not letting up.

*****

Jake peered into the dark and sleeting rain that had increased in intensity since they turned off Interstate 5 for the Washington coast.

Keeping the wandering 1980s-era RV within the faded lines on the curvy road took both hands on the wheel. He had been driving for two days straight, with only a short night of sleep. Having fun with place names kept him awake.

"Gizzard, population 25? Who would name a wide spot in the road, Gizzard?"

"I don't know," said Ruby, distracted as she bunched up her leather coat for a pillow against the passenger door in the RV. "Maybe it's a family name."

"Oh, you mean poppa Gizzard, momma Gizzard, and baby Gizzard?" Raising his voice into a false soprano, he added, "Oh, little Gizzy, you're so cute; you look just like your father, a chicken organ."

"Maybe it's a French family." She pounded the jacket into a ball, using more force than was necessary, annoyance creeping into her voice. "Not 'Gizzard,' but 'Giz-zard,' with emphasis on the second syllable."

Jake was about to say, "Oh, I'm riding with an English teacher," but his thoughts were cut short by flashing red lights piercing through the unrelenting rain. A deputy waving a flashlight in front of barricades blocked the road.

Jake's sudden braking jarred his passenger. "What's this? Is that a cop?" She pulled the jacket around to cover her face as if sleeping.

To slide open the driver's side window to talk to the

deputy, Jake first had to pull out the Dollar Store rubber-tipped spatulas he had jammed between the sliding glass panes. The noise deadening felt between the panes had worn out on the old RV long ago, chewed up by the blasting Arizona sun. The constant rattling of the glass panes against each other caused his head to throb. It was either the spatulas or a steady supply of Ibuprofen.

"The highway is blocked," shouted the deputy. "You'll have to turn around and go back, maybe to the little diner about 10 miles back. They will have hot coffee."

"It's too narrow for me to turn around," Jake shouted. "We can wait here and make our own coffee. Say, what happened?"

"It's an accident, and a bad one, too." Water ran off the brim of the deputy's hat. "There've been a couple of accidents tonight, so aid cars are slow in coming."

"Was anyone hurt? Can we be of assistance? I should have extra blankets." Jack reached down to pull up the handle to open his door.

"I couldn't find the driver when I arrived. No other living person is here."

"No other living person? Were there fatalities? What happened, anyway? And what's blocking the road?"

"I can't tell you anymore," the deputy shouted above the downpour, "you'll have to stay right here until we get this cleaned up." Waving his bright light up ahead, the beam caught three large white crates on the road and an older motorhome, half on the road, half off.

"Let me take a look. I'm a reporter. You may have seen my byline in the *Seattle Times*." Which was true but not precisely accurate.

When the young deputy paused, undecided about what to do, Jake opened his door and hopped down. Sure, he'd get wet, but a story is a story. And he would need a good story where he was going.

"I wouldn't go down there; you don't want to see that,"

shouted the deputy, which in Jake's experience, always meant that's where the real news was.

Switching on the flashlight option of his iPhone, Jake followed a pair of tracks in the muddy shoulder made by something veering off the road. Aiming the light higher through the pelting rain, he saw the overturned RV nose down in a pond — a toy hauler in RV terminology, with a cargo compartment in the rear, made to carry sand buggies and other playthings.

The cargo door had sprung open, but instead of ATVs, he saw the three crates — which, when he got closer, he realized were chest freezers — dumped across the slick road.

"Ouch!" Jake slipped on the wet grass lining the muddy edge of the roadside, banging a knee on a large piece of rubber tread debris. Steadying himself on the first freezer, the lid fell open, and out sprawled an arm, shoulder, and head of a body. A human body.

Spraying his light inside the freezer, Jake saw the rest of the unclothed woman. Then another body underneath her. Then another.

CHAPTER 2

Monday morning, Jake was feeling rough after the long night at the accident scene as he introduced himself to the staff of the Long Beach *Beachcomber*.

They weren't feeling so chipper, either.

A week ago, the fresh-faced new owners of the community newspaper were killed in a tragic and baffling highway accident. The couple in their 30s had come to town only six months before, after a decade each of working at Portland's prominent metro newspaper, full of energy and ideas on interjecting new life into Long Beach's stodgy and soggy community newspaper.

Gone were the ads on the front page, blurry headshots, and press releases masquerading as news. In their place were large, dramatic photos, authentic stories about the people of the half-dozen coastal communities the weekly paper covered, and a caring concern on the editorial page on how to energize the local economy while treasuring the specialness of the place.

They also knew how to sell in an age when "everybody knows print is dead." Revenue of the paper had popped as circulation and ads surged.

That ended on a foggy night, and now Jake was here.

Three days ago, he was renting a park model home in a Yuma RV resort where he was 30 years younger than the other sun-bleached residents, enjoying lazy walks under bright blue skies to a small diner in the mornings and then to a locals' bar in the afternoon for happy hour.

He was getting by just fine on the severance received when laid off from Seattle's major newspaper — when management decided kids who knew how to create clickbait were more needed than veteran editors who knew how to check facts. It helped, too, that the kids were paid half of Jake's salary.

On the past Friday, Jake was continuing his journey through local beers — trying a Jailbait Blonde from Yuma's Prison Hill Brewing at the locals' tavern — when his iPhone vibrated on the bar.

The number was not one Jake recognized, so he let it ring again. Still, it was a Washington state number — perhaps an old buddy also caught up in the layoffs. Worth a try. He slid, "accept."

"Yeah?"

"Jake Stewart? This is Dave Raymond. I understand you have just spent a year editing a weekly newspaper in Arizona. But you are through with that now?"

"Yeah..." The past year flashed through Jake's mind: the woman who, in the end, dumped him, finding a fortune in lost gold but then turning it over to the state, solving three murders, saving a small newspaper when both the editor and then the publisher were part of the body count, and then being rescued himself by a pizza delivery driver who styled himself as a "soon-to-be-famous" novelist.

"But," said Jake as the bartender slid another Blonde his way, "I told everything to the police. Are you an investigator?"

"Oh gosh, no." The man at the other end laughed. His voice had the throaty quality of old age, but the tone was light. Friendly, drawing Jake in.

"I have a job for you. There is an urgent need for a man like you here in Washington."

"Ah, I already have a job. I'm working on my second Jailbait Blonde today." Jake took a sip. Maybe this beer was just a little too fruity. His eyes ran down the chalkboard listing today's beers, looking for something a little more like a beer and less like an umbrella drink.

The voice paused, not knowing how to take Jake's comment about the blonde. Jake didn't see any need to clear up the confusion.

When the voice started again, it reeled Jake in with a story. And Jake was always a sucker for a good story. He was a newspaperman through and through.

Dave Raymond explained he was a newspaper broker, helping people buy and sell small community newspapers. Six months ago, he sold a bright young couple the 120-year-old newspaper in Long Beach, Washington, in desperate need of revitalization. The energetic, personable couple — Miles and Jane McKinney — started quickly. But then they were killed a few days ago in a mishap.

"They left behind two little boys, one seven, the other four. The couple spent all of their savings buying the newspaper. It's all the inheritance the boys have. If the newspaper doesn't come out every week, it will lose the authority to run legal ads, about a third of the paper's income. Without legal ads, the paper will die, and the boys will have nothing."

Ah, sweet Jesus. The story had its effect on Jake. He pushed the Blonde back across the bar.

"How soon?"

"Can you leave today? The staff is in shambles, and it doesn't look like next week's edition is coming out."

After discussing the details with Dave, Jake stood up to return to his rented house to pack.

At the entrance to the RV resort, someone had parked a near-vintage motorhome — a dated box on wheels, aluminum siding painted green and yellow, missing hubcaps, rusted bumpers, and a few dings and dents. The "for sale" sign suggested $4,500 and gave an address in the resort.

A house on wheels — at a cheap price — might just be what he needed, as tourist towns like Long Beach can be expensive places to live.

"Does she run?" Jake asked an old guy who shuffled to the door on the second knock.

"Does she run? She's a beauty. Hums down the road, unlike these modern RVs with their environmental controls and power doodads that break and cost a fortune to fix. I've thrown in all the dishes, bedding, and gadgets any RV needs. My motor homing days are over."

When Jake offered $4,000, the old guy grabbed a bill of sale and registration from a table near the door, signed where he was supposed to, and closed the door in Jake's face without even looking at Jake's check.

In a day on the road, Jake made it about 650 miles to just south of Sacramento, where he spent the night at a rest stop.

As the old man had suggested, the RV, which Jake named "The Incredible Hulk," purred along I-5 north at a safe and sane 60 mph in the slow lane. Any faster, the rig shuddered and shook until Jake feared something would fall off, having already experienced the loss of one windshield wiper.

The Hulk didn't miss many gas stations. Having plenty of time to think behind the wheel, Jake wondered how a travel book called *Seeing America, One Gas Station at a Time* might sell. Probably not well.

At Red Bluff in Northern California, the winter sun was replaced by clouds, and by Grant's Pass on the entry to Oregon, the clouds started leaking.

After Portland, the rain picked up in earnest and had not quit to Long Beach.

Arriving in Long Beach in the early morning hours after being let through the accident scene, Jake moored the Hulk in the newspaper's parking lot. Part of his pay package, he presumed, although Dave hadn't been too clear on exactly what that package might consist of.

Looking for at least a short night of sleep, Jake suggested, "I can make up a bed by lowering the table and moving around the cushions, or you can sleep on the sofa. It's short, though."

She looked at him for a long minute, no expression on her face, as if sizing up his intent. "I'm fine in the passenger seat."

"Nonsense. It's nothing. These RVs were made to sleep

half a dozen people." Jake nudg,
the table and went to pop it from
out of it when — *crash*! The table fe.
dangled from the wall.

Ruby laughed. And laughed. Th
their meeting dissolved.

"OK, I'll clean that up later. There shou.
blankets in these overhead compartments." But, i.
plastic bins full of outdated canned food, books, ↄ
jigsaw puzzles. Lots and lots of jigsaw puzzles.

Ruby stared at Jake, then looked towards the rear .
Hulk. "We're adults. There is a queen-sized bed with blankeι.
can sleep above the blankets in my clothes."

"It's like a 1930s Clark Gable - Claudette Colbert movie,"
laughed Jake, waiting to see if she got the reference to *It
Happened One Night.*

She did. She smiled.

After a few minutes, she said, "I'm a little cold. And I
don't want to wrinkle my clothes by sleeping in them. They are
all I have. Can I join you?"

Being adults, at first, they kept their distance. But then
they didn't. Being adults, they knew what to do and how to do it
for mutual satisfaction.

The stress of two long, hard days on the road, plowing
through heavy rains, then finding bodies in freezers all melted
away in the warm touch of a zestful woman. Sleep came late for
Jake, but it came easy.

d loose the wooden pedestal on
ts wall holder to make a bed
to the floor. Metal braces

awkwardness from

be some extra
lust dishes,
hes, and

he

l of bodies spread
ht be the top story
chance to mention
net the staff in the

might be the best story of the year."

"Great. But first, let me make introductions. I'm Jake Stewart; I've been asked to run the paper until new buyers can be found after the sudden deaths of the McKinneys. I haven't even had a chance to read back issues or learn who is who. So, you are…?

"John, John Ryan. I do the beach beat and human interest stories. And boy, do I have a good one."

John was about Jake's height but with hunched shoulders. He looked beyond 70, and some of those 70 years were likely spent at various saloons, as his age-spotted face was an explosion of blood vessels. A rounded nose and large ears — ears do keep growing as we age, thought Jake — gave him a bloodhound look. A lop-sided steady grin said here was a guy who didn't take the world too seriously.

"Yep, and it's a damn good story, too." John turned and walked to one of the Army surplus metal desks in what Jake took as the newsroom if a newsroom can be three metals desks, each with a couple of chairs covered in well-used cushions, piles of papers on the floor, padded dividers heavily studded with pinned-up phone numbers and news articles.

Yes, thought Jake with bemusement. John's a storyteller

from the barrooms who knows how to throw out a story with a hook and then bait listeners to ask for more.

We all have our roles to play, thought Jake, so he played his. "John, tell us. What's the story?"

"Two words: A talking dolphin."

Jake's inner proofreader noted three words, but John didn't look like a reporter who let pesky details trip up a good story.

"A talking dolphin? You have the story written?"

"Just as good. It's all right up here," John rubbed his bald, sun-spotted head. Slipping a reporter's notebook into the back pocket of his tan dungarees and tucking in one shirttail of the thin plaid shirt, John threw a rain mackinaw around his shoulders and walked for the door.

"Wait, don't you want to write the story now? We will lay out the paper tomorrow and get it printed Wednesday. I need to see what we have in hand."

"Gotta make my Monday morning rounds. People are expecting me." And John was out the door.

"Oh yeah, expecting him. Like expecting him down at the Green Hornet."

Jake turned towards the speaker, a woman not five feet tall, with short graying hair and silver glasses on a lanyard around her neck. She was wearing a bulky knitted green sweater with an image of a white cat on the front and black yoga pants. Maybe she didn't have a full-length mirror at home. A nameplate on the desk she was standing next to read Pat Carnation.

"What's the Green Hornet?"

"It's the oldest bar in Long Beach, and the patrons look like it."

She had a way of speaking, standing sideways to Jake while looking past him. He caught himself a couple of times glancing over his shoulder to see if someone else was standing there.

"I have a pretty good story this week, too," said Pat.

"Oh…"

"A 45-year-old woman hiking the beach trails on Saturday went to use one of the state park pit toilets. She accidentally dropped her iPhone in the poop pit. She then worked off the toilet seat to reach deep into the vault but slipped on the wet floor while leaning over the edge and fell in."

"Oh my god!"

"Yeah, right, huh? But she did get her phone and called for help. The first person she called was her boyfriend, who said, 'Not with a 10-foot pole.'"

"She next called 9-1-1, and the fire department came, broke down the locked door, and pulled her out. But not before I got there. I keep my police scanner on all the time. I have photos of the rescue and an interview with the woman."

"That's wonderful! What did she say?"

"She was very practical after getting over her initial embarrassment. She said the phone cost $1,300 and contained many personal photos she didn't want to lose. Her hiking gear — I held a fire department blanket around her while she stripped it off — cost maybe $100, even with the boots. She could shitcan the clothes — pardon the pun — and still come out way ahead."

"Did she get any of the… ah… poop anyplace it shouldn't be? Was she worried about infections?"

"I drove her in the blanket to my house, where she took a long, hot shower. She stood under the water so long that I brought her a glass of white wine and later gave her some clothes. I dropped her back at her car at the beach parking lot. She intended to go to a motel for the night. I think she is done with the boyfriend."

"That is a pretty hilarious story. Have you written it?

"Yes, I have. Now, we need a headline. How about Ker-poop!"

"Brilliant," laughed Jake.

Jake looked around the office to see three women talking in a small alcove off the main room.

"I'm up next," said the shortest, hopping up from her rolling office chair. She had close-cut hair, a thick face was probably about 40 years old, and collected her weight around her stomach and rear. She had been collecting for a while.

"I'm Bing, and I'm the person keeping this place alive."

"Nice to meet you, Bing. Keeping this place alive…?"

"Yeah, I do billing, bookkeeping, subscriptions, special sections, and run the book publishing side." She had come up a little too close to Jake, like his personal space was hers, too.

"The book publishing side…?"

"Yeah, didn't anyone tell you? Along with putting out the *Beachcomber*, we publish books. Book sales and special tourist sections are the secret sauce that lets the rest of you play at newspapering."

It was hard to dislike a person in the first minute of meeting them, but in Bing's case, Jake was willing to try.

"I first learned about the *Beachcomber* three days ago," he said. "I know almost nothing about the people here or the community. My job is to keep the *Beachcomber* in business until it can be sold, so the young children of the McKinneys will have some inheritance. Can I assume you are on board with this plan, too?"

"Might take a while to find more suckers like the McKinneys," said Bing. If a person would say, "tut-tut," she came very close to saying it with her look of disdain.

"Really? It seems like the McKinneys were doing well."

"Jake, dear, there are five primary drivers of the local economy: timber, fishing, construction, tourism, and cranberries.

"Environmental laws have killed timber and fishing, tourism is dead because of the recession, construction is also hurting because who builds in a bad economy, and rustlers are crippling the cranberry farmers. Newspapers ads are the first place local businesses cut when cash flow dries up."

"Wait, what? Cranberry rustlers?"

"Ask one of your reporters. Oh, and a woman is coming in shortly to talk to you about a book she wants us to publish. Get ready." She walked to the desk nearest the front counter to pick up the phone as it started to ring.

Two more employees to meet. They have to be more normal than the first three, thought Jake.

The first of the two was named Brandi, a cute if horsey dishwater blonde about 20 years old. She said she had spent two years attending nearby Grays Harbor College, getting an Associate of Arts degree in graphic design. She was desperately looking for a graphics job in Seattle, but in the meantime, she was back living with her mother in the same bedroom she'd had since first grade. She designed the ads.

The last woman turned out to be both the newest and the oldest employee. Her name was Adele. She was a tidy, slender, professional woman in her 70s with medium-long gray hair held to the back with a silver clip. She had been the ad saleswoman for the *Beachcomber* but had retired when the McKinneys bought it, and Jane, with her flashing good looks and beaming personality, began selling ads.

Adele had returned with the deaths of the McKinneys, and she told Jake she would stay until he found someone else. Sooner would be better than later, she said, but two days back, she had discovered a renewed joy in the social interaction from making sales calls in the community again.

"I tried ad sales for a few weeks," remembered Jake. "It was a nightmare."

"Oh, Jake. Treat them like children," said Adele, laying a hand gently on Jake's arm. "Believe half of what they say, and steer them in the right direction. Over time, you'll be rewarded. Or, they will go out of business, slink out of town, and you'll be here to gloat."

CHAPTER 4

"People sure carry guns in this town."

"What do you mean?" Jake was chopping up the rib-eye steak into cubes for his favorite dinner of seasoned steak bites prepared in an air fryer and served with half a dozen savory dips.

He had made a quick shopping trip during lunch to clear his head after the whirlwind of the last couple of days and meeting the staff in the morning.

He needed comfort food after his first day on the job. What an odd group at the newspaper, but newspaper folk were often out there. It was difficult to tell whether they were made that way by the job or came to the job because they were odd.

Seeing the Incredible Hulk — his home — waiting for him in the newspaper's parking lot brought a smile to his face when he had left the office after work, and then finding Ruby inside doubled it.

"About half of the men who came into the restaurant today had guns strapped to their waists. Then, I served the pie to four women at a booth and saw the butt end of a pistol sticking out of one of the women's purses. And the funny thing was when she saw me notice the gun, she didn't move to cover it up."

Ruby had figured out how to repair the dining table from last night's collapse and sat with her legs curled up on one of the table's padded bench seats.

"I have no problem with guns. I've been around guns, and I've been around people with guns much of my life. Guns are a tool. I'm good with that. But like any tool, they take care and caution. You don't just hand a chainsaw to a 60-year-old grandmother and expect her not to cut her foot off.

"Some of the guys didn't look like they would know much about using a gun in a pressure situation. I asked my new boss, Amber, what was happening, and she said Beast Man mania had gripped the town. Weird."

Jake dug a potato from the cabinet below the sink, then grabbed a second one. He decided to pair the steak bites with French fries, also to be made in the air fryer he had bought at the hardware store. Lots of healthy French fries — no grease, no heavy smell inside the RV.

"So, back up. You got a job today?"

"Yes," said Ruby. "Waitressing at a diner on the main street called — wait for this — Ruby's Diner. I think they hired me based on my name. It's a cash-under-the-table job, but that suits me just fine." She was sipping red wine Jake had pulled out from a built-in wine rack. The Hulk was old but had its touches of faded luxury.

"I bought that at one of the gas stations I stopped at before I picked you up. I call it 'Gas Station Red,'" said Jake, waving the bottle at Ruby, inquiring if she wanted a refill.

"'Picked me up.' I don't know if I like that expression. Besides, I think I was the one who picked you up." She smiled and stretched her glass towards Jake.

After their night together, Ruby relaxed around Jake. She smiled, laughed at his lame puns and jokes, and leaned into his passing touches. However, she brushed aside any questions about her past. Not unpleasantly, but making it clear she wasn't going there.

Jake forked the seasoned steak chunks into the heated air fryer basket and then turned to cut the potatoes into fry slices.

He figured he would cook the steak bites first and then, while they rested, toss in the fries. Maybe start another bottle of red to make a nice dinner, hoping for a happy ending. However, Ruby didn't appear to be a woman who needed a couple of glasses of wine to do what her body wanted to do anyway.

Bang, bang, bang! Knocking exploded at the door,

causing Jake's pour to jerk astray, spilling drops of red on the table. "Jake, there's a fire at the mill!" shouted Pat from outside. "Grab your rain jacket. Let's get photos for this week's edition!"

*****

On the way to the fire, Pat explained as long as she had been a reporter at the *Beachcomber*, the mill was a hit-and-miss affair. Running often enough to keep some men in town employed and eligible for state unemployment benefits but closing at every dip in lumber prices or new environmental regulations.

"I know the family. They're good people," said Pat, racing along the wet, twisty country road to the mill site a few miles from the town. Rain splattered the windshield, and water flew from the puddles she plowed through.

"But it was inevitable the mill would go away. All the best logs are being shipped to the Orient at prices impossible for local operators to pay. The Far East is swallowing up even second-rate timber."

"Has the cause of the fire been determined?"

Pat gave Jake one of her sideways glances. "I'd say it was sparked by the friction of a fat insurance policy rubbing against the owners' desperation. But, nothing has been suggested yet on the police scanner."

She turned off the pavement into the mill's rutted, muddy parking area and was out her door with camera in hand before the car's engine died.

Jake saw a night sky lashed by waves of brilliant red and yellow flames through the windshield heavy with raindrops. He had seen enough fires to doubt a volunteer fire department could save the mill.

Stepping out of the car, his right foot sunk into a deep muddy rut. When he yanked his foot up, the mud sucked the sneaker from his foot, causing him to lunge forward, his stocking foot stepping into the goo.

"Damn!"

"Jake, get bystander comments while I take photos!" Pat shouted as she ran towards the fire.

Jake gave up on fishing out his shoe, jerked a reporter's notebook from his back pocket, and limped over to a couple of men in heavy jackets.

"Any idea what caused this?"

"It's those damn hippies!" said the first man, water running down the sides of his canvas cap. "They hate us for earning a decent living!"

"Hippies died out in the '70s. It's the greenies!" shouted the second man over the sirens. Water dripped off his long, white beard hanging to his chest.

"It's those vagrant vets," said a third man approaching from behind Jake. "They are destroying this town. Let's shoot them all!" His hand rested on the butt of a holstered gun, protected by a mud-spotted Navy pea coat.

Remembering what Ruby had said about people with guns, Jake decided he would try a different group of bystanders.

"I was one of the first here," said a woman in a plastic see-through parka and rubber boots. "I live just down the road and heard a loud explosion. I ran down here, and already flames were 50 feet high. Maybe somebody bombed the mill."

She switched her iPhone back and forth between vertical and horizontal views, the camera's strobe flashing through the night. The rain had matted her dark hair, but other than occasionally wiping drops off her forehead, she didn't seem to notice the wetness.

"That explosion was probably the sawdust in the waste burner. Fine sawdust can collect in the air in confined spaces and be explosive." The calm talker was a trim man in his 50s, guessed Jake, with a clean-shaven face, glasses, and yellow rubberized rain gear.

"Do you work at the mill?" Jake asked.

"Hardly anybody works at the mill. But I know the logging business — I used to be a timber cruiser."

"Timber cruiser — I don't know what that is."

"I would walk an uncut block of timber, and based on the size of the trees and their number, I would come up with a value. In the 20 years I did that, I have walked nearly every hill and valley in the mountains around here. But, no more, no more. Not after what I have seen." His eyes turned down as he shook his head back and forth.

Jake edged closer to the talker, trying to hear over the frantic sounds of the firefighters, the roaring fire, and arguments — inexplicable to Jake — breaking out among spectators. Screaming sirens from freshly arriving fire trucks from nearby departments made conversation almost impossible.

Moving his head to within inches of the talker, Jake hunched over to shelter his reporter's notebook and pen. "Like what?"

"Well, like this. One morning, I got to a site in the mountains early because I had a couple of jobs that day. I was working my tape measure, making notes in my log, and stepping off the plot I was there to cruise when I emerged into an area that had been previously clear-cut.

"There were only stumps remaining, and on one of the stumps was a woman, a naked woman, just sitting, staring at the colors of the dawn.

"Nobody lived around there. It was all owned by the big timber companies or private landholders — no houses at all. And there were no cars on the logging road where I had parked. I was startled to see her — and of course to see her without any clothes — I asked if she was OK.

"She slowly swiveled her head towards me — she couldn't have been more than 15 feet away — not taking her eyes off the sky. Then, bang, her eyes flashed on me. She stared for a few seconds, a cold stare — not frightened or alarmed — then turned her head back to the dawn sky and sat perfectly still."

"Wow. Weird."

"Yes, and to be perfectly honest, one man to another, sights like that could have kept me going back. But other things I saw later, over the years... I quit that work. I'm never going back into the woods, I'll never walk those hills again. I shiver now just talking with you. Sometimes, in the early morning hours when I can't sleep, my mind goes back... but I never will."

"Jake, come on! I got my photos." Pat suddenly appeared at Jake's other shoulder. "We got to go. I left my daughter home alone.

"Hey, what happened to your shoe? This is no place to be walking around in stocking feet... you'll catch your death of cold."

CHAPTER 5

"John, where's your story on the talking dolphin?" On early Tuesday morning, Jake had made the short walk from the Hulk, still in the newspaper's parking lot, to his desk to start laying out this week's edition.

He had taken a moment Monday afternoon to glance at last week's paper — which the staff had put after the owners' accident — and saw why newspaper broker Dave Raymond was so anxious to get Jake on the job.

The story about the publishers' deaths was at the top of the front page. The rest of the tabloid-sized front page was filled with a story about new library hours, a press release from Waste Management about new garbage rates, and the start of a long, dull article on the high school marching band director.

Jake had counted eight typos — the two worst in a teaser headline for a story on page 3: Breast man has inflamed pubic.

It didn't get any better on the inside pages.

Between the shambles of the paper and from meeting the quirky staff on Monday, it was clear a professional newsman was needed if the *Beachcomber* were to stay alive.

Jake was just that man.

In almost 20 years of working at Washington's most prominent newspaper — including four years part-time as he went through journalism school at the University of Washington — he had moved through the sports beat, then fire and cops, courts, city government, a couple of years at the state capitol Olympia, a short while on the business beat until he had gotten the paper sued by a prominent developer who claimed Jake libeled him (the paper won the case, but transferred Jake to another beat) and then the last few years as metro editor where he oversaw coverage of the city in general.

Then, the past year, after being downsized by the *Seattle Times*, he kept a small-town Arizona paper alive after the local sheriff's wife killed the owner.

By the time reporter John Ryan finally lumbered into the office at 9:30, Jake had roughed out the front page of the *Beachcomber* and planned most of the rest of the 24-page edition.

Jake gave John a few minutes of rumbling around the office, filing a Styrofoam cup from the office's coffee pot — yelping when he spilled a little on his hand — then slopping coffee across the room back to his desk when he tossed down one reporter's notebook, picked up another before tossing it down again.

He wore the same clothes as yesterday, looking like he had slept in a lightweight plaid shirt, tan dungarees, rain mac, and beat-up hiking shoes.

After he had stared off for a moment, not moving a muscle, Jake figured it was time to ask him about the dolphin.

"The talking dolphin? Oh, that's a good one, all right. And getting better each time I interview him. But, I figured with the fire story, your story on the freezers full of bodies, and Pat's tale of the woman who fell in the toilet, the front page is covered.

"You know... let me get some pictures, and I'll have the story for next week." John rose carefully, slipped a reporter's notebook into his rain gear, and rambled to the door.

"Out to get some pitchers at the Green Hornet is more like it," Pat muttered loud enough, intending Jake to hear.

"What's John's story anyway?" Jake asked her. "He seems a little... out of it."

"He washed up here about ten years ago, and the previous owner — old man Corcoran — took pity on him. He was always giving people second, third, and fourth chances. John is not the worst character. Corcoran helped out by any means."

"Where did he come from? He seems like he has been a

reporter. He knows how to stall an editor."

"Yeah, when I say 'washed up here,' I mean that. He was a features reporter for the *Oregonian* in Portland when he sold them on an idea of an adventure series, showing how one man — maybe the last man on earth — could survive in the wilderness. He got it in his head that this last man would build a raft from wind-fell saplings and work his way around coastal inlets, living off the bounty of the land and sea.

"Of course, it was all a fabrication. He spent most of his time living off the bounty of one coastal bar after another, sending in made-up dispatches of his days of roughing it. The series was a big hit, though, and the newspaper turned a blind eye to verifying John's accounts. John is an excellent writer who can carry a good story along.

"Then, one day, I don't know why, maybe too much alcohol, John decided to prove to himself his story was possible. He found an old canoe along the beach, and paddled through the surf, feeling the 'siren call of the mariner, ' as he later said, salt water spray stinging his face, that sort of thing when a big swell from a passing cargo ship tipped him over into the water.

"He was fortunate. He had made it to the shore, lying among the oyster and clamshells, gasping for breath, when Corcoran found him during his morning beach walk.

"John got fired from the *Oregonian*, but Corcoran offered him a job here, and he's been here for the past ten years."

"Does he produce any copy?" Jake wondered, thinking the paper could use a sports editor who also covered the cops, courts, and fire beat. Maybe trade a charity case for one of those kids just out of J-school who would work cheaply.

Pat twisted her mouth into a grimace. "John is very popular with readers. His stuff is… how to say it?… out there. John was clickbait before the term clickbait was invented."

*****

Jake worked the rest of the day helping Pat shape her

mill fire story, editing the copy that had come in earlier, writing headlines, sizing photos, laying out the paper, and in quiet moments, trying to flesh out his own story on the mystery of the bodies in the freezers.

"We have not yet been able to ID the bodies. But, we don't think there was any foul play involved." Undersheriff Snyder had a monotone delivery in talking with Jake over the phone, but what he said was outrageous.

"No foul play? I saw three freezers, all of which were full of human bodies. I don't want to alarm people, but if we have a serial killer on the loose, we have a duty to inform our readers. And where's the sheriff? Why aren't I talking with her?"

"The sheriff is busy running down the Beast Man of the woods. But that's another case. We've taken the nine bodies from the RV to the morgue. None of them have any marks, except those that occurred during the accident. They all look like they died of natural causes."

"Natural causes? Somebody stuffed nine bodies of people who died of natural causes into freezers and was out driving them around in the back of an RV? What does the driver say?"

"We haven't found the driver yet."

"Have you looked in the swamp the wrecked RV was nose down in?"

"That's not a swamp. That's a cranberry bog along the edge of the highway."

"OK, cranberry bog. Have you looked in there yet?"

"The owner won't let us."

"What? The owner won't let you? Bog, swamp, it's still a potential crime scene. Who cares what the owner says?"

"If we saw a person suspected of criminal activity run into the bog, then, yes, we could go after him. But, otherwise, the bog is private property, and we can't search there without a warrant."

Then undersheriff Snyder added, "You probably don't know this, but the bogs are filled with water at certain times.

Disturbing the water will damage the crop. So, the sheriff has decided not to push the issue for now."

Jake had what he needed for the first week's story on the bodies. His reporter's instincts told him this story would have legs and continue to be page-one material for weeks. Far better than a story on new hours at the library.

"You shouldn't expect the sheriff to be too aggressive at disturbing the bog," said Pat, as Jake was muttering after he had hung up the phone. "She was elected with cranberry money."

CHAPTER 6

"So, I told them, 'You damn kids. When your dad sees this, he's going to crap a blue bean.'"

The bartender was busy fuming to another patron down the length of the well-worn dark wood bar, which allowed Jake to look around at the Green Hornet, apparently the bar of choice of local old-timers.

Many "no's" were pinned to little signs here and there. No cashing checks, no dancing, no bathrooms except for customers, no circus dwarfs, no spitting, no gambling, no working women, no dogs, no caulk boots, no crude language, and no motorcycles. Jake thought the Green Hornet must have been quite a place at one time to make these rules necessary.

What grabbed the eye, though, was the one element that stood out, the one thing Jake had never seen in a bar before, or anywhere in his years on earth, was a six-foot mannequin wearing a green bee costume. The appearance was halfway between a cartoon — bugged-out eyes, antennae with fuzzy black balls at the end, and a beer drinker's gut — and something from *Invasion of the Bee People* with a long stinger curled threateningly around from the back to the front.

Someone had placed the mannequin inside a clear acrylic box on the back bar counter and then leaned the box forward, held by cords, as if the bee might be lunging toward customers at the bar.

Wow, thought Jake, I've heard of people seeing damn strange things *after* they had too many drinks, but here, before the first drink, you likely saw the most bizarre sight you'd see all day.

"Yeah?" The bartender had left her conversation to stand impatiently in front of Jake.

"I see you have Mac & Jack's," Jake tilted his head at the line of beer taps just in front of him. "I'll have one."

When she started the pour, Jake offered, "I used to date a woman who knew the Mac of Mac & Jack's in high school. She said he was a brilliant guy."

"Well, la-de-da. Five bucks, Mister Hollywood."

"Take it easy on him, Velma. He works with me." A hand clapped Jake on the shoulder as John Ryan slid onto the next stool.

"You're not much better," the bartender, who was apparently named Velma, sniffed. "This better not become a newspaper bar."

"John, I haven't seen you all day. So, what's the deal with the bee man up there?"

"That's quite a story, Jake, quite a story." John clinked the ice cubes around his short, otherwise empty glass, looking off in thought.

Jake got the hint. "Velma, how about hitting John again on me."

"Yeah, it better be on you. It ain't going to be on me." She had started filling a new glass when John sat next to Jake, knowing what was coming. She banged the honey-hued glass, took Jake's $5 bill, and left again.

Jake allowed John his first taste and switched to asking what he had been up to all day.

"It's a big one." John ran a hand over his head. "Not the big, big one, but a big one."

"The talking dolphin?"

"Bigger than that, Jake, bigger than that. Not that the dolphin's not a blow-your-sox-off story. It'll go national. But this one is a little bigger, a little bit darker. Something you don't want to talk about when others are around."

The comment caused Jake to reflexively swing his eyes around the darkened bar where he mainly saw single drinkers, mostly old, with inward soulful stares.

Only one table exhibited signs of life, three young guys laughing, showing each other their cell phones, fist bumping between swallows of beer.

Jake swung his head back and was about to ask John for more when John interrupted him.

"You were lucky the other night. Very lucky. Out there, on the highway, in the rain, dark, late. It's not a good idea to get out of your vehicle."

"At the accident? Other than slipping on the wet bank, banging my knee, and then getting a fright from the bodies in the freezers, it seemed safe. A deputy was there."

"Yeah. This county has lost deputies before." John took a long drink.

"So... what? Bigfoot?"

"Pffft. Bigfoot? There's no Bigfoot. That's just a joke made up for the tourists. No, the real danger out there, on the dark rainy night on the deserted road...." John lowered his voice and moved his rubbery lips toward Jake's ear, "...the real danger is the killer fog that comes up out of the forest. Some are saying that's what happened to the McKinneys."

"What? Killer fog?"

"Yeah, unbelievable, right?" John paused to take a drink. "Fog can't kill."

"I wouldn't think so."

John took one last sip of melted ice, teasing out the last of the alcohol. "It causes you to go deaf, and you can't see anything. That's when the Beast Man comes at you.

"Well, I'm off. I got a couple of people to talk to and stories to get. Good luck with your first edition." John peeled off his stool, tightened his rain slicker, and was gone before Jake could respond.

One of the young men left a moment later.

*****

Ruby was waitressing an evening shift at the restaurant, so Jake decided to stay for another beer to congratulate himself on one exciting week.

Seven days ago, he had plucked a ripe lemon from a tree in Yuma, where the skies were brilliant blue every day, the temperatures in the mid-70s, and the only excitement was watching jets from the nearby Marine air base scream overhead, sometimes dipping so low to almost shake the fruit loose from the citrus trees.

Now, he was editor of a paper he hadn't known existed — the savior editor, apparently — the owner of a lumbering box on wheels, sharing a bed with a beautiful yet mysterious woman, and hearing wild tales of killer fog while seeing dead bodies in freezers, all the while living in a land of perpetual rain.

"Hey, when does the rain stop?" he asked Velma as she slid a Mac & Jack's his way.

"It's not raining."

Jake turned his head to the two windows flanking the single door into the bar — neon beer signs were lit up the panes that didn't appear to have been cleaned this century.

"I see water running in waves down the windows."

"That? Pffft. That's nothing. That's rain residue."

"I agree with you, mate," came an accented voice from his side. "We've been here since last fall, and I think it has rained every single day. I feel the itch of mushrooms growing on my back."

Jake turned to his left, where one of the young guys from the table was waiting to pay his tab.

"I've seen cars with thick coats of green algae, blankets of moss on every side of trees, houses rotting into the ground, cows stranded on little islands in the pastures, water gushing off buildings into streets, creating puddles so wide you need a boat to cross.

"And the people. Everyone is in rain gear. I think they must have two modes of dress here: heavy mackinaws for winter, lighter rain slickers for summer."

Jake laughed. "You're depressing me, man."

"You know the cure for it — another beer."

Jake laughed again. "You guys look a little young for this bar. What are you doing in town?"

"We're in innovations and old ideas with new twists." Laying down a $5 tip for Velma on the bar, he snapped up his rubberized green raincoat, donned a canvas slouch hat, nodded bye to Jake, and headed for the door.

"I wonder what he meant by innovations and old ideas with new twists?" Jake mused to himself as Velma came by.

"Him? Australians. You can't trust the buggers." She slid the tip into the pocket of her baggy smock and continued down the bar, picking up empties.

CHAPTER 7

The next day — Wednesday — was press day. Usually, Bing took the pages to the press, but Jake wanted to see the operation, so he rode with her the 100 miles to Vancouver, where the daily's newspaper plant printed surrounding weeklies.

These were hard times for city newspapers. The Vancouver newspaper was no longer a valid daily — now publishing only four days a week — and now pushed the line that an enhanced website was better than the feel of newsprint in readers' hands.

A dangerous argument in Jake's mind. Once you sent readers to the internet, would you ever get them back to newsprint?

Before the great recession, the Vancouver paper had splurged on a new press from Germany that could print full color on every page. Unfortunately, hard times and bankruptcy followed, but the German press — true to its craftsman heritage — still churned out beautiful colors.

Now, even the littlest community papers — like the *Beachcomber* — could have full-color eye-popping graphics, photos, and full-color ads on every page.

With his big-city experience, Jake aggressively approached color and design. To survive, newspapers had to wow readers into looking their way, and Jake believed they still could.

He had chosen to run only one photo of the mill fire on the front page but made it the entire width of the page. Red and yellow flames flickered into the black sky, contrasting with deeply shadowed faces of firefighters standing idle, overwhelmed by the destructive power of nature.

On page three were four more fire photos, plus the story that continued from page one — a dramatic package.

A newspaper isn't just two pages — this edition was 24 tabloid pages, and Jake tried to put a "hook" on each page, either with a headline or picture … something that would catch a lazy reader just thumbing through.

Jake subscribed to the roadside diner style of journalism. That's where a guy comes into a diner, orders a cup of coffee, and while he waits, turns to the fellow sitting a few stools away and says, "You wouldn't believe what I just saw down the highway." Those following words are what should be in the newspaper — every issue.

It did help that Bing and Adele had sold a six-page President's Day sales section. That left Jake with 18 pages to fill, and after a couple of pages for classifieds and legal ads and two for high school sports, not such a challenge.

What was a challenge was listening to Bing nonstop on the drive to Vancouver.

"So after I returned the shoes to Amazon the fourth time, I tried to find a human to complain to. Amazon does not let you talk to a human. And what's the point of complaining to a robot? But I didn't even get to talk to a robot. I could only send an email. And who reads an email? A robot?"

Jake found few pauses to interject his own words, but he tried when she slowed for a deer crossing the road.

"Your paycheck comes from local businesses. Maybe you should buy local."

"Buy local? Nobody buys local." She honked to hurry along the doe and her spotted fawn.

True, thought Jake. Fewer people are buying local, and newspapers are dying because of it.

"I can't believe the Mormons who moved in next door have so many noisy kids…." Bing was off on another in her long series of complaints about how the world was wronging her.

*****

For Jake, the joy of newspaper work was its combination of intellect and craftsmanship.

It takes an agile brain to respond to news and draw out information from sources, artfully weave those facts into stories that make sense and craft them into a compelling newspaper edition.

Like a fine woodworker making a beautiful piece of furniture, every detail had to dovetail into the next. A poor cut, noticeable sanding marks, or sloppy application of the finish would ruin the product's final glow.

For a newspaper, a mistake on page 7 could spoil the entire edition.

Which was why Jake was looking at page 7 now the printed newspaper was back at the office. And which was why Adele, Brandi, and Pat were frantically going through the 2,000 copies of the paper, turning to page seven.

Somehow — and no one took the blame — a quarter-page ad for a going-out-of-business sale for Tom's Drugstore announced discounts of 50 percent would begin Friday.

According to Adele, this was the biggest ad Tom had ever run, which might help explain the going-out-of-business sale.

Moments after getting the issues back to the office, Tom had come by to see a proof of his ad.

He went apoplectic. "Wait! I didn't know the ad was running this week! I thought I would see a proof for next week's ad. That discount doesn't happen until next Friday. I can't be telling people now I'm having a sale next Friday. I want them to buy at full price now!"

Jake apologized to Tom but said since the paper was already printed, there was nothing they could do. Maybe he could start his sale a week early?

"And lose all that full-price revenue? I can't do that! But

now, people will come in Friday expecting a big sale."

While Tom was squealing about a financial disaster, Jake's eyes happened upon Bing's desk, where he saw a dater stamp and a pad of red ink. She had been sending overdue notices with a "pay by" date in red ink for drama.

"Tom, how about this? We'll go through each edition and stamp next week's date in red next to Friday. That way, people will at least know when the sale starts."

"If that's all you can do, OK. But I'm not happy."

Jake had dispatched Adele to Meredith's Stationery to buy more dater stamps, and now the newspaper staff was busy stamping Tom's ad on each page seven with next Friday's date.

Before leaving, Tom announced: "I'm not paying for this ad, don't even think about billing me."

"Naturally," soothed Jake.

"I'm not paying for next week's ad, either!"

"Naturally not."

Tom pulled rubber gloves from his pockets, buttoned up his parka, and left, saying, "This would never have happened when old man Corcoran was here."

"As if he ever advertised when 'old man Corcoran' had the paper," said Adele, and the whole staff laughed, feeling the tension ebb away.

CHAPTER 8

The following day, Sheriff Pam Ramblewood stopped by the office. "I should take you for a ride in the patrol car some time," she offered.

Jake jerked at the suggestion, his mind racing through the last time he rode in a sheriff's car on the way to a murder scene when it looked like he would be the one murdered.

"Front seat or back?" Jake asked. She laughed. She had come by the *Beachcomber's* office to introduce herself to the new editor — the sheriff's position being elected, an intelligent sheriff knew friendly relations with local media were good politics.

Sheriff Ramblewood — Jake was impressed the local community was progressive enough to elect a woman to the position — apologized for not taking Jake's call about the bodies in the freezers.

"What have you got on the bodies so far? Are they murder victims?" Jake sat at his computer, bringing up a new screen to take notes. "Are you calling for help from any other agencies? Or the FBI?"

The sheriff shook her head. "As Undersheriff Snyder said, early indications are these people were not murdered. It's something else, but we don't know what yet. The county coroner is examining the bodies. We'll know more in a few days.

"And I would prefer not to have inflammatory speculations about murderers on the loose. You might have noticed people in town are already on edge," said the sheriff. "We've been having trouble with some of the mobile population, and there are lots of rumors about break-ins, thefts, even unreported murders."

"What did undersheriff Snyder mean when he said you were chasing down the Beast Man of the woods?"

"Oh, that." Sheriff Ramblewood tugged her gun belt higher. When she turned away momentarily to listen to a speaker on her shoulder, Jake had a chance to look closely at her. She was short, maybe five-two, not heavy, 45-ish, blonde, in a tan shirt and pants.

She constantly pulled up her heavy belt, weighed down by her service revolver, pouches of spare ammo, a hand radio, and handcuffs.

If there were ever an argument for a female sheriff carrying a handbag, she was it. But a tough image was part of the resumé of a county sheriff, and a purse didn't look as tough as a gun on a leather belt around the waist.

"I just got a call about a Beast Man sighting. Want to go along?"

"You bet!" A Beast Man story for next week's front page? Jake jumped at the chance, quickly buttoning up a rain slicker he had found on the office coat rack — probably belonging to the departed Miles — and grabbing his reporter's notebook and camera phone.

The patrol car squished through rivets of rain draining across the pavement as Sheriff Ramblewood steered with one hand, frequently turning to Jake to explain how the county had long drawn its share of unsettled people.

"Some people headed west in wagon trains," she said, "until they found the perfect piece of land and put down roots. But some kept going, always expecting something better over the next mountain. Or they kept going to put further distance between themselves and the troubles of the past.

"The Pacific eventually stopped the most driven, the most footloose, and the most lost. But while they may have settled in their bodies, their minds were still unsettled. So, here in Pacific County, we've always had our characters, our lovable loonies.

"Only today, it might be lost veterans from Vietnam or, more recently, the desert, or mushroom foragers who carry long knives and kill each other over secret, high-value mushroom locations, or meth heads who steal anything and everything to support a habit that is burning holes in their brains."

"Which one of the groups does this Beast Man belong to?" Jake thought about taking notes but decided hanging onto the grab bar above his head was better. The sheriff was a fast driver.

"Who knows? Who knows if there even is a Beast Man? A book was published last year — by your newspaper, by the way — with local history. It retold a story from the 1910s about an escaped mental patient who inhabited the woods north of here, killing hikers, hunters, and fishermen. He was called The Wild Man of the Olympics.

"Somehow, that legend caught the public's imagination. Every minor crime, juvenile runaway, or spouse gone missing was attributed to this reincarnation of the Wild Man, now called the Beast Man.

"Till now, we have a Beast Man problem. Only I think the problem is the public's imagination has gone wild, not some fuzzy guy haunting the forest."

Sheriff Ramblewood pulled off the highway to bounce over a dirt road. At the end appeared a farming operation with a giant rectangle pond in the middle.

"You can lock the doors and stay in the car if you like."

If Sheriff Ramblewood was issuing a challenge, Jake was up for it. "I'm good," he said, opening his door. "What kind of self-respecting wild man would be caught in this downpour anyway?"

This time, he watched where he put his foot to avoid a puddle, then started walking around the pond — or bog was the proper word — in the opposite direction as the sheriff.

Huge raindrops fell so hard on Jake's rubberized hood that he couldn't hear any other sound. And water flooded down his forehead into his eyes when he tried to look up — holding his hand out as a rain visor.

Deaf and blind, he stumbled along the walking path around the bog when suddenly huge prints of a naked foot appeared in the mud. He stopped, startled, and reached under the slicker for the phone to take photos.

"ARRAGH!" A roar pierced the gloom. Jake looked up just in time to see a large figure charging, catching him off-guard. The force of the impact carried him into the bog.

Cranberry vines wrapped around Jake's head and entangled his legs as the creature roiled on top of him, pushing him further underwater. His eyes stung from the putrid pond water, his mouth sucked in a gulp of foul liquid, and his lungs screamed for air.

Jake's hands found a muddy bottom, and he realized the bog was only a couple of feet deep.

With a twist of his shoulders and a turn of his hips, learned from years of competitive wrestling in high school, he rolled from under the creature. This surprised the attacker, who fell back and tried climbing up the side but slipped back into the bog. With a roar, he clambered to his feet, charged the side again, and this time was up and out of the bog and disappeared into the rain.

But not before Jake got off one photo of his fleeing naked backside.

"Jake! What are you doing in the bog? You could be harming the farmer's property." Then Sheriff Ramblewood saw blood mixing with the water running down Jake's face. "Oh my god, what happened?"

*****

"I can't tell if that's a man or a beast. Is that his wanger or a cranberry vine dangling there?"

Bing was carefully studying the photo — with Brandi looking over her shoulder — after the printed papers returned from the press, just like every other reader would be doing when the *Beachcomber* was delivered.

If Sheriff Ramblewood had hoped to win Jake over as an ally in her public relations efforts to tamp down the fears of town, just the opposite happened when on the following week's front page of the *Beachcomber*, Jake published his blurry photo of the fleeing attacker.

Jake was careful in his account of the incident not to use inflammatory adjectives or labels, such as Beast Man or creature, and not to be overly dramatic about being catapulted into the cranberry bog.

But that wouldn't damper speculation. Or soothe the town's fears.

"I will say, Jake, since you have come to town, the quality of the news has picked up," said John, holding one of the freshly printed papers in his hand. "Makes it hard for another reporter to crack the front page."

"Speaking of that, John, where is the story on the talking dolphin? This town could use a good talking animal story about now."

"That story just keeps getting better, Jake." John turned his face sideways, a half-smile as though remembering a long-ago joke.

Turning back to Jake, he lowered his voice. "But I'm chasing down something bigger. Something you would be very interested in. Very interested. Because you were there at the start. Well, maybe not the start, but early on."

"Look, John. I haven't seen a story from you since I've been here. I know I'm only a fill-in editor until new owners come along, but I still have to look at the overall efficiency of this small operation. We can't keep running one reporter short."

"In truth, Jake, quantity has never been my thing. Quality that's my style. And when you get a John Ryan story, readers will be talking for months. Maybe years."

"I hope this is not some type of 'government conspiracy' story with no bottom to get to and no hopes of ever seeing print."

John stepped closer to Jake, put his arm around the editor's shoulders, and gently turned him towards the large office windows to the outside.

"Oh, there is a massive government cover-up, and I'm well into running it down. See all that rain out there... but that's a story for another time. What I'm working on is a 'meat-and-potatoes' crime story with dark, sinister undertones. Well, what you saw the other night in those freezers is just the tip. The tip of the iceberg."

CHAPTER 9

Another edition out, another late waitressing shift for Ruby, another visit to the Great Hornet for Jake.

Ahhh. The first sip of a cold Mac & Jack's. In a world full of clutter, incessant talkers, and constant imperfections, here was something perfect he could curl a hand around.

He wrapped his fingers around the pint glass firmly, not wishing for them to slip on the condensation forming on the cool drink, and was bending his elbow to his mouth when his iPhone on the bar started bouncing.

Jake glanced at the phone, then at Velma, who pointed sternly to the "No cellphones" sign taped to the acrylic box holding the bar's namesake.

Looking around, Jake saw a small vacant table near the men's room at the back. Moving there, he hit the table's wobbly pedestal with his knee as he sat down, knocking the first foamy sip of the day from his glass onto the Formica top.

He didn't believe in omens, but still…

He slid "accept," and a quiet voice entered his ear. "This is Dave Raymond. Can you talk?"

"Sure," he told the newspaper broker. "I'm just here with my friends, Mac and Jack. I left you a message earlier asking about the progress in finding new owners for the *Beachcomber.*"

"I was visiting my grandchildren on the East Coast the past week. As I told my son if I had known how much fun grandchildren were, I would have had them first." A long laugh followed.

"But you are advertising for new owners… calling past interested parties, neighboring newspaper owners, getting the word out, right?"

"I have not had much success with advertising in the past. The problem with today's world is you get a lot of tire kickers who don't have any money."

"How about advertising in the Seattle *Times*? Maybe somebody like me who is being downsized out of a job would jump at the chance to be an owner instead of a clickbait producer in this new world of journalism."

"That's an idea. But few big city newspapermen want to move to the boondocks. Or work that hard for an uncertain paycheck."

"Hey," Jake put his glass down. "Speaking of a paycheck. What is the status of my pay? You were vague the last time we talked, and I felt sorry for the kids. And I've seen so many newspapers die. I didn't want to let another die if I could help it. But, we all like paychecks."

"Lawyers are still working on the McKinney estate. Courts take time. Lawyers and accountants are deal-killers, in my experience. They don't work on deadlines as we do. This one time, I had a group of five newspapers — three weekly newspapers and two companion shoppers — all but sold when this accountant...."

"Wait, wait. I can see the *Beachcomber* would be a sweet property for some couple, maybe with a couple of kids who wanted to connect with nature but still have cities not too far away. I think you should advertise the hell out of it."

"Oh, OK. I'll look into that. Have to run, I've supposed to FaceTime my grandkids in a few minutes. Keep up the good work, and try to make a profit. A profitable newspaper is always easier to sell."

Jake put his cell phone down next to the beer glass, and the condensation was gone.

Mac & Jack's is only great when cold. Even "good" might be too strong when it's warm.

Ah, what the hell? Compromise is the way of the world, thought Jake, and he lifted the beer mug to his lips.

CHAPTER 10

"I am probably the whitest person you have ever seen."

The woman, slender, likely in her mid-60s, sitting across from Jake's editor's desk was indeed white. With all these clouds spewing rain, so was every Caucasian inhabitant in town.

She had introduced herself as Barbara, with an Eastern European last name Jake hadn't entirely caught. And she had come to talk about having the *Beachcomber* publish her book.

Bing had told Jake just a little about the book publishing side of the business, but he had been so busy juggling all the balls to keep the little weekly alive he paid scant attention.

So when Jake came into the office this Thursday morning and Bing told him he had an author waiting for him, he didn't know what to expect. Bing had hinted book publishing was profitable for the paper, though, so he thought he should hear the author out.

"My book is about a Black jazz musician who lived in New York in the 1950s but toured Europe and most of the U.S. Not so much the South."

"Hmmm. I believe a good writer can write about anything, but there does seem to be blowback these days on white people telling the stories of Black people. Maybe you should find a topic closer to your life."

"This was my life. Well, not really. But let me explain." Barbara reached into a substantial old-fashioned lawyer's briefcase sitting in a small puddle of water running off her shoes on the floor and drew out a manuscript.

"I'm the fourth generation of my family who has lived here, and I went to the same high school as my mother and aunt. I had a career teaching English at the same high school. My mother found a log truck driver to marry, and they made a life here, but my aunt, this was wa-y-y-y too small of a town for her. She bolted for New York when she was out of high school.

"This was a few years after World War II, so young people made the rounds from New York, Paris, and Berlin. These were the beatniks, the hipsters. Everything seemed possible. War had destroyed the old constructs, and a new spirit of freedom had been released.

"By the early 1950s, wartime bebop's nervous energy and tension were replaced with cool jazz. The sounds that one day would make Miles Davis, John Coltrane, and Herbie Hancock household names were already percolating in the small clubs. 'Be cool, man' was the password.

"My aunt, Aunt Billie, immersed herself in this musical milieu so far from the backwater town on the Pacific Ocean she had grown up in.

"And she found a guy, a jazz musician — a horn man.

"In New York or Europe, a white woman with a Black man was part of the scene. Not here in Long Beach. She seldom returned home but sent us long, colorful, detailed letters of life almost impossible for a little girl like me to imagine."

Barbara stopped speaking, caught up in the past.

"OK," Jake prompted. Thursday morning, the day after the issue is printed, is like Monday morning, the start of a new week and a time for grand thoughts of mighty possibilities for the newspaper. But still, trips down memory lane by old-timers could easily chew up a morning.

"Yes, OK. So here is the deal. My mother died recently, and when I was cleaning out her stuff, I found this collection of notes, like a diary. It was written by my aunt's guy, a horn man of some repute named Artie Sayles. I sat at my mom's little kitchen table, among the residue of my mom's long life in her Long Beach home, and was transported to a different place and a different, magical time.

"I'm not a jazz person. Rolling Stones is more my kind of

music or Linda Ronstadt. But I could hear the music in my head as I read Artie's pieces.

"I would like to turn his writing into a novel. He would be the central character, my aunt his companion, and famous and not-so-famous jazzmen passing in and out.

"What do you think?"

Jake looked up to see Bing adamantly shaking her head from side to side.

"Well, Barbara, I'm still new here, but my first thought is you need a bigger publisher than us, a more sophisticated publisher. We're the *25 Places to (Maybe) See Bigfoot in Long Beach* type of publisher."

Barbara sighed and slid the manuscript back into the briefcase. "Sure. I thought you would say that, but I wanted to try. And, I must say, just telling you the story has inspired me all over again. In my author's notes, I'll include you as my favorite rejection." Thanks.

*****

"Glad you got rid of her. That would be a terrible book." Bing had bounced over to Jake at his desk where he was standing after shaking Barbara's hand goodbye.

"Besides, I have the best idea ever for the paper."

Jake was about to object. He had been drawn into Barbara's story about the 1950s jazz scene and how a sheltered girl who grew up in Long Beach could flow through that scene. The next time he saw Barbara, he might suggest she change the point of view to that of Aunt Billie, using the notes from the jazzman to add color and depth — and soul.

For now, he asked Bing, "What's this great idea?"

"It would be a rant-and-rave column. But instead of asking people to mail or email their comments, as some papers do, we would set up one of the office lines to record calls after hours. People could call in about what they are mad about — or happy with — easy-peasy."

Leaning a little closer to Jake, taking up even more of his personal space, she added, "And it would take up some of the slack from John's lack of stories and your own distractions. I could even edit it. We could call it 'Bing's Bitches.'"

"'Bing's Bitches'? I thought it would be a rant-and-rave column. Not just complaints." Jake took a step back, bumping into his desk.

"Oh, sure. There could be some raves, I suppose." Bing moved forward. "But people like best to complain. And the fact they could do it anonymously and get it out for the public to see... it would be a huge hit. It could fill up pages. You could eliminate those yawner school board and city council meeting stories."

Again, Jake thought to protest. The bedrock of local newspapering was informing the public on the activities of the government and schools.

Instead, he said, "So, you wouldn't require names from the callers? I can see libel and factual issues. What if a caller said his neighbor was beating his wife or the school principal was abusing children?"

"Great idea! We could have another column, 'Bing's Bounce Backs,' where the people could call in to deny what was said about them. People would *love* this! You could dump most of the high school sports stories, too. Who wants to read about girls playing softball or sweaty wrestlers rolling around on mats?

"And," Bing moved even closer, waving her hands in Jake's chest in excitement, "you might get leads on actual interesting stories. Like maybe crimes going on or Beast Man sightings. This could be so good!"

Oh, no, thought Jake. This was a terrible idea. Newspapers had specific rules, and one was to fact-check stories. Unfiltered gossip was the domain of the internet.

But it's true, he always read rant and raves columns in other papers, and he would be the final editor so he could stop egregious material. Maybe this idea could work... and would get Bing to back off.

"Typing the transcript from the phone calls would be laborious. Are you up for that?"

"The iPhones have an app for that, dummy. I would play it for my phone and it would transcribe the words. I suppose I could clean it up and remove any profanities — the newspaper is so fussy about swear words."

"And libel concerns? What would you do about that?"

"Who is going to sue us? The newspaper is practically bankrupt anyway. They can't get oil out of a dead fish. And — oh, oh! — a lawsuit would bring us attention, getting even more readers of Bing's Bitches!"

CHAPTER 11

The only rain gear Jake had found at Garrett's Hardware when he had gone shopping to keep dry was a fluorescent yellow jacket with broad orange horizontal stripes — it made him look like a road crew worker.

But maybe that was a good thing, he thought as he slipped his arms through the coat to get out of the office and away from Bing.

Years ago, a gruff newspaper veteran told him that "newspapers had lost their soul when reporters started being paid so well they stopped carrying lunchboxes to work."

Jake had been a young reporter then, so he thought being paid well enough to go out for lunch was an uptown idea.

Just like going out for lunch sounded like a great idea now.

Walking along Long Beach's main shopping area nestled to Highway 103 that runs up and down the peninsula, he dodged sandwich boards advertising little cafes and coffee shops. He paused at a tourist shop window plastered with posters announcing an upcoming kite flying competition. Motels, a few dating from the mid-last century, were still hanging on among their newer, upscale cousins geared to spenders from Seattle.

When Jake and his friends had turned 16, a buddy purchased a rusted-out Triumph car from the 1960s. Jake, the driver, and two other friends had piled into the convertible for a guy's road trip from their Seattle suburb to the beach.

It took a few hours to get to Long Beach, but the car was thrilling to handle around corners on the two-lane highway to the beach. Or so the buddy said. He didn't let anyone else drive.

In town, they cruised the main drag, eyeing the girls walking the strip, the girls watching back four guys in the spring of their lives in an English sports car with a bad muffler.

One of the shops placed a dummy on the sidewalk, wearing a t-shirt saying, "F.B.I."

It was odd, Jake had thought, to sell shirts advertising the FBI until — thanks to the slow traffic on the jammed strip — he could read the fine print: "Female Body Inspector."

Today, this tourist shop had the same shirt design in the window. Jake chuckled. Bad taste never goes out of style.

Waiting for a light, he looked ahead at "The World's Largest Frying Pan" as part of an outdoor museum exhibit.

Seeing the frying pan got him thinking about food, and looking around the intersection, he saw a red building on the corner with a giant razor clam on the roof. "Clam chowder served all day," announced a neon sign in script lettering in the window.

Perfect. And so was the name: Ruby's '50s Diner.

"Can I sit where you can service me?" Jake asked when he saw Ruby adding up a bill at the front cash register when he got inside.

"I don't know, cowboy, what kind of tipper are you?" She smiled back at him.

"I can't think of any comeback that doesn't sound too risqué for a family place like this," he replied. "So, where is your section."

"I could have my own ribald comeback, but for now, I work the booths. Choose any one of those." She pointed at a line of a dozen booths with '50s vintage upholstered seats in shiny burgundy and silver "V" backs. They were in waterproof vinyl. In this town, they had to be.

Elvis' *Blue Bayou* was playing in the background with its wistful lyrics: "I feel so sad, got a worried mind, I'm so lonesome all the time since I left my baby behind, on Blue Bayou."

Perfect for the dreary day outside.

Sheriff Ramblewood sat with undersheriff Snyder at the

only other occupied booth. Both had handheld radios next to their plates.

Jake nodded at her, but he purposefully chose a booth a few tables away. Being a newspaperman, he wouldn't be able to help himself from listening to their conversation, and today, he wanted time off from the news.

"I'll have the chowder. Can you take a break to sit with a customer?" Jake asked when Ruby came by with a menu.

"Well, as you can see, we are pretty busy…" she scanned the ten empty booths, "…but for a randy newspaper editor, I think I can make an exception."

She left to place Jake's order, suggestively shaking her long ponytail as she walked away.

A beautiful woman with an easy, fun personality who likes to play with words, just the woman for a newspaper guy, thought Jake. Even though they met by chance at a gas station, maybe there could be a future…

A sudden eruption of the police radios caused Jake to jerk around to see the sheriff and deputy spring up from their table, grab the radios, and head for the door. "We'll get you later, Ruby," said the sheriff.

"What's up?" he asked as she hurried by.

"There's been a murder at the cranberry bogs."

CHAPTER 12

On Friday morning, it was still storming outside.

"The sound of rain pitter-patting the roof makes me want to snuggle under these warm blankets."

Ruby moved her backside closer to Jake, getting his attention. Sure, it was a workday for him, but when a woman in bed says she wants to snuggle, only a fool would think about work first.

Jake was no fool.

Besides, his commute was only 100 feet — from the Hulk still in the parking lot of the *Beachcomber* to his desk. No wasted moments driving into work for him. Although, now that he thought about it, maybe he should start up the Tacoma in the next few days. He hadn't run the pickup since coming to town, and he didn't want it to get rusty.

Ruby shifted her body again, and Jake turned to matters at hand.

*****

"Mr. Editor Man." A loud knock came at the front door of the RV, along with more shouting. "Mr. Editor Man. I need to talk to you."

Jake climbed out of bed, pulled a pair of jeans over his bare body, and slipped on a black t-shirt. One convenience about living in the RV was the closets were tiny. Not a lot of time was wasted choosing which clothes to wear. If it was clean yesterday, it was clean enough for today.

Jake opened the door to see a short woman standing at the steps. She looked vaguely familiar — 40 to 50 years old, thick sour face on a robust frame. Water ran off her no-nonsense short graying hair.

Bing… this woman looked like a copy of the newspaper's office manager.

"Can I come in? It's damn wet out here."

Jake glanced back at Ruby, who gave a "who cares" shrug of her bare shoulders, then turned her face away while scooting under the blankets.

"Sure. It's, uh, a bit of a mess."

"I've seen worse… I guess," she said, looking around, wrinkling her face. "I see you have everything here… stove, fridge, table. Toilet in the back, right? Does this nice little home on wheels have a coffee pot?"

"Uh, we have a Keurig that makes a single cup at a time."

"Black is fine for me. If I wanted to drink milk and sugar, I'd have a milkshake. However, Bill and Bea's drive-in does make an espresso milkshake. God help the people who drink it."

The woman wedged her way into one of the bench seats at the table. "I don't suppose you have a donut, do you? A cake donut goes great with my morning coffee. Not one of those surgery-glazed things where the flakes fall off on your chest. These things catch enough as it is." She brushed raindrops from her bosomy front.

"Sorry, no donuts. I need to go shopping today." Giving way to the inevitable, Jake dropped a coffee pod into the Keurig, filled the water reservoir, and pushed the brew button.

"My sister said you would be here. She said you were always late coming to work on Fridays. Big night, huh?" She glanced toward the unmade bed where Ruby lay still.

"Anyway, my sister is Bing. Maybe you saw the family resemblance? All the sisters are almost clones of each other, although she is the sweetest of the bunch.

"My name is Mary Teresa. And I have a problem that you need to solve." Looking around, she asked: "I'd take a muffin with peanut butter and a sprinkle of sugar, or one of those foreign bagels, if that's how you roll."

"Well," said Jake, still standing, "before I make you breakfast — and have Bing notice that I am ever more late than usual — how about telling me why you are here and what problem I should solve for you."

"Jeesh. I'm not expecting breakfast. Only something friendly put on the table to have with my black coffee if that's not too much for you."

Jake again gave in to the inevitable and pulled a toaster down from its home in a cabinet over the sink, found two English muffins in a plastic bag, and dropped one into the toaster. He pulled a jar of peanut butter and a box of sugar from another cabinet, which he placed on a plastic placemat along with a knife in front of Mary Teresa.

He also placed a freshly brewed coffee before her and started a cup for himself. He wasn't sure, but he thought he heard muffled laughter from the bed.

"Now, why are you here?"

Mary Teresa looked at the toaster. "I don't like them burned, but not soft, either. Crunchy. Tight to the bite."

"OK. But really, why are you here?"

"Well... Bing has probably told you all about me, but to clear up any misunderstanding, let me start at the beginning. I have often noticed in her stories she is not very accurate. It's a wonder to me she is working at a newspaper."

The muffin halves popped up. Jake displayed the toasted sides to Mary Teresa, who nodded, then served them on a paper plate. He took his coffee, in which he had poured a packet and half of Splenda and a dollop of Half and Half, and sat down on the other bench seat.

Taking a heavy breath, Mary Teresa started talking.

"I live on the family farm. It's 40 acres a few miles inland, bordering federal timberlands. My grandfather had a small sawmill there, and when the old-growth trees were gone — and he couldn't steal any more from the feds — he started a dairy. My dad had the dairy all the years the sisters and I were growing up."

"Just you and Bing?" Jake wondered.

"We were four of us, but we lost one."

"Oh, I'm sorry to hear of her passing."

"I didn't say she had died. I said we lost her. She joined one of those loony cults around here, run by some old Russian named Rasputin. Big beard, big hair, a big ego, and an eye for the ladies. They all live in a big house over by Raspberry Slough, where they 'commune with nature,'" Mary Teresa shook her hands, making air quotes. "I don't know what they live on, maybe wild gooseberries and marsh reeds, because I've been by once or twice, and they are not much for vegetable gardening."

Feeling hungry herself, Mary Teresa tore apart one half of the muffin and jammed it in her mouth.

"So, as I was saying," when she could talk again, "there's no money in dairying, and dad sold out when the feds offered to buy the cows from small farmers. That was only a few years before he died. As the oldest child, I was left the property."

She stopped to add more sugar to the other half of the muffin.

"As I said, the farm borders federal land. A few years ago, after those terrible wars way over there in the desert — why anybody lives there in that heat, surrounded by sand, I'll never know. Why we had to send our boys over there... well, anyway, some fellows who saw too much came home only to find they didn't fit in anymore. Many drifted to rural parts of the state where they weren't surrounded by people nagging them to get a job, settle down, to 'get over it.'

"Lots of these guys, maybe hundreds of them, perhaps thousands, hunkered down on federal property, living in camps in the woods, only coming to town for food or — the lucky ones, some might say — to pick up disability checks.

"You know, it makes me so damn mad that everyone puts up signs to 'Support the Vets,' right? But when a homeless vet stands on the sidewalk in front of your store or sleeps down the street from your home in a vacant lot, they're on the phone to the sheriff, demanding the police move these bums along."

Mary Teresa noticed her plate was empty. "Did you say there was another muffin?"

"Yeah. I'll fix it. You keep talking."

"Well, I was no better than these other good citizens. When I saw strangers in camo jackets and Army packs crossing the back of my property, I shouted at them and honked my horn. One time, I even waved my Dad's shotgun. I called the police more than once, only to be told if they were doing no harm and not threatening me, the police wouldn't come out.

"I'll be honest," said Mary Teresa, spreading a thick layer of peanut butter on the newly toasted muffin, "this inaction by the cops really teed me off.

"The next time I saw a lone guy crossing my property, I took out after him. I marched across those 40 acres, my Wellies stomping through the wet grass, my coat flapping, and steam coming from my ears. I might look like a gentle person, but when I get mad, I can be intimidating."

Jake did not doubt that.

"But, maybe it was the energy I spent huffing across the fields, or maybe when I got up close to the guy, I saw a ghost of a man — bent, thin, gaunt face, eyes that wouldn't meet mine.

"So, instead of chewing out his butt, I asked a few questions and heard his story. It was heartbreaking. He said he was the class president at his small high school, a football player, a straight B student, and always had an after-school job to help out his single mother. He had joined up just after graduation to fight for America, but, well, war isn't how it's advertised.

"Now, I know, I know. He could have just been BS'ing me. But looking at him, hearing him talk, and seeing his thin frame shiver in the cold tore me apart. And I'm not a person who falls for a sob story."

Jake did not doubt that, either.

"I returned to the house, brewed a big pot of coffee, grabbed some day-old donuts, dug out some luncheon meats, and took them out to him."

"That night..." Mary Teresa's eyes went wet, and her

voice wobbled, "... That night, I decided to leave a large urn of hot coffee the following day on a little table at the back of my property, with some cold cuts for the guy. Or any other guys passing on their way to camps deep in the forest.

"I did this every day, and I started noticing a few guys milling around the table in a week or so. Maybe I'm the world's biggest sucker, but I have a portable patio canopy I put up during the summer in my backyard. I took that out there to provide shelter. Some of the guys helped me set it up. And I talked to them, and their stories were different, but all the same, too.

"I've done that for months now."

"Wow!" said Jake. "That is some story. It would be great for the *Beachcomber*."

"I don't want a damn story about me. That's not what this is about." Anger flared across her face.

"You know the same sheriff's department who wouldn't come out earlier when I called? Well, they are all over out there now. Oh yeah, they are. You get some dead cranberry farmer, and little Miss Cranberry queen from 1995 gets a hard-on to arrest a homeless vet.

"That's the story I want you to do... how the sheriff's department is harassing homeless vets while the real killer is laughing."

CHAPTER 13

"He isn't just some dead cranberry grower. He was my uncle. So, yeah, I am pressing this investigation hard. If that means rousting some homeless vets, so be it."

Sheriff Ramblewood's fiery eyes glared at Jake from across her wide wooden desk, accepting no challenge. Except for her animated face, she looked tired. Undersheriff Snyder looked no better, slumped in a hardback chair at the side of the sheriff's desk.

Jake had dropped in Monday morning to get an update on the murder and the bodies in the freezers case and to share Mary Thersa's concern about harassing veterans.

"OK, maybe that was a little harsh." The sheriff turned away and then looked back, inhaling and blowing a big breath. "We don't get a lot of murders here. In the ten years I've been with the department, we only had one other murder, which was a tourist-on-tourist thing over a kite. And yes, it was as odd as it sounds.

"But, in the last few months, something has changed. There's a different air, a different, more violent, scary vibe. Nothing you can put your finger on, but it's there. And it's not just me — every officer in the department is feeling it on patrol."

Undersheriff Snyder nodded his head in agreement. "Coastal communities can be tough places," he said. "You must be tough to be a logger, fisherman, or construction worker. You kept a civil tongue because the guy next to you knew what to do with his fists.

"Now... half the population is packing guns. Even the meekest mouse of a guy, or the smallest woman, becomes a raving lunatic behind the barrel of a handgun. When officers go out now on a disturbance call, they have to watch for guns being pulled. It hasn't happened yet, but we fear it will."

"The *Beachcomber* is certainly not looking to inflame the situation," said Jake after a flurry of note taking. "But for us to do our job — to report the news fairly and dispel rumors — I need the facts about what happened to the farmer and what investigations you are following. An aware public can help you. A scared public will only get in your way. There are already plenty of rumors about this being a Beast Man attack. Anything to that?"

"This murder has absolutely nothing to do with the Beast Man," said the sheriff, looking directly into Jake's eyes. "I've asked undersheriff Snyder to prepare a press release on everything we are willing to share about the murder. Bill, give it to him."

Damn, a press release, thought Jake as he held out his hand for the paper from Snyder. That means all the local media is getting the same information, including the Vancouver daily newspaper 100 miles away. While Pat had photos of police at the cranberry bog murder site, readers of the *Beachcomber* expected more than every radio station and the regional dailies had.

Jake quickly scanned the release. "I see you have the who, what, where, and how — ouch, a wooden scoop to the back of the head, that's an odd murder weapon — but I don't see a why."

"Darrell, Darrell Green, as the report says, was a third-generation bog man," said the sheriff.

"He was a history buff and had a little, private museum in one of the old barns. Had restored tractors from the 1930s and '40s, collected old harvesting machines and tools, and framed blown-up photos of the harvesting operation on the walls. He'd put on presentations for school kids.

"My first fundraiser was held in that barn when I decided to run for sheriff. Darrell was the one who pushed me to run when the old sheriff was photographed accepting a personal favor from a woman tourist who didn't want a speeding ticket.

"The murder weapon was from Darrell's museum. It was a long-handled scoop, kind of like a shovel. Growers used to agitate the bogs when the berries were ready and then scoop them up as they floated to the top.

"Did Darrell have any enemies or competitors who might have snapped?"

"No. All the growers sell to Ocean Spray, the big corporate powerhouse in the cranberry universe. The little guys, and they are almost all little guys, help each other out. Cranberry growing is a tough business with a tiny profit margin. If the growers didn't work together, none would make it."

"So, no new brash young upstarts trying to revolutionize the red berry world?"

Undersheriff Snyder made a barely audible throat-clearing sound.

Jake caught it, and so did the sheriff.

She looked sharply at Snyder, then drew a breath in.

"Darrell's son, Bobby, and a few younger growers have turned to organic cranberries, selling outside of Ocean Spray. Organics are big now with all the suburban moms. These growers — only a few — sell at Pike Place Market in Seattle and other farmers' markets. The prices are higher, but person-to-person retailing requires more work and some charisma. And Bobby's got charisma to spare."

"So, what's the problem?"

"Remember, Darrell is... was a history buff. In local cranberries' long, complicated history, chemicals saved the industry when disease devastated the crops 100 years ago. Now, cranberries are accused by the greenies of having the most significant pesticide risk per serving of any fruit or vegetable.

"Darrell and the other older growers dispute that, of course, and have cut way back or switched to safer sprays, but the organic guys played up the pesticides when selling their products.

"That created quite a bit of tension. I don't believe

Darrell and Bobby have spoken in years."

Sheriff Ramblewood said she had to run. She'd let Jake know of new developments at the appropriate time.

Jake got in one more question about why officers were rousting vets.

"They have been taught how to kill, haven't they?"

*****

"Larry says he's sorry."

Jake was composing the first few paragraphs of the murder story in his head after leaving the sheriff, waiting for the traffic light across Highway 103 to change, when the softly spoken sentence came floating his way.

He turned to the left, but nobody was there, he turned to the right, and a big guy was hunkered inside his oversized Army surplus coat. He had a 1,000-yard stare into the gloom of the morning. Jake hadn't seen him earlier, but he was still replaying the interview with the sheriff. Maybe he had been at the corner when Jake walked up.

"Did you say something to me?"

"Larry says he's sorry. He thought you were poachers. Larry likes deer. He doesn't like poachers."

Street people were common when Jake lived in Seattle, and so were their strange conversations. Between grunge-inspired tech geeks talking on invisible earphones and loonies conversing with aliens, it was hard to tell when someone was trying to make a friendly conversation versus being off their meds. Technology was making us all look like nuts.

The best tactic was to keep your eyes straight ahead and move on quickly. Damn, these lights were slow in Long Beach. Jake was about to jaywalk when the voice said, "The Sarge said you are OK. That's why Larry is sorry."

The light turned green. Jake stuck out one foot, then pulled back.

"Wait." The person in the green coat had already turned

down the sidewalk. "Wait," Jake said louder.

"You were talking to me. Larry is sorry? What is Larry sorry for? Larry is not the person who attacked me at the cranberry bog, is he? Why was he naked? And, who is this Sarge who says I'm OK?"

"Larry was bathing. The bog is warmer than the mountain streams."

The man was half a head taller than Jake's five-foot-ten but looked doubly large because of the thick field jacket and double pair of pants — one pair of ragged fatigues with holes in the knees over another — and a patched-up pack on his back. His black Army boots showed scuff marks and scratches.

"The Sarge. She gives us coffee. She is nice to us. She talks to us."

"Coffee. Good idea. " Let me buy you a cup of coffee..." Jake saw Ruby's Diner just behind them, "... here at the diner. We can sit in the warm out of this rain, and you can tell me your story."

"No. Too many people."

"Sure, OK. How about this? I'll run in and get coffees, and we can talk... there, near the go-cart track on that bench. I want to know more about Larry and the poachers."

Jake dashed into the diner. "Ruby, quick, give me two coffees in to-go cups. I'll pay you later."

When he returned to the street, the big man had disappeared into the mist.

CHAPTER 14

"Jake, some kid wants to talk to you about a book. When you get through, I have great news about Bing's Bitches. So, hurry up with him. He's at your desk." Bing pointed with a tilt of her head as if Jake didn't know where his desk was.

"Hi, you have a book idea you think we should publish?" Jake settled into his padded office chair. So far, aspiring authors seemed long-winded. May as well be comfortable.

"This is the BEST book idea ever! Well, maybe not ever, but plenty flippin' good." The kid looked like a high school senior and introduced himself as Levi. Just Levi. "I only go by one name," he said, explaining it would be easier for the book-buying public to remember.

"OK," said Jake, knowing a story was coming.

"So, you've read sci-fi books, right? Where aliens invade earth, and they're so smart, right? Like the '90s movie *Independence Day* where they know how to use our technology against us, know where the military bases are, and have these super-duper weapons that destroy cities with just one ray, right?"

Jake didn't feel any need to slow Levi's flow by speaking.

"OK, but how real is that? Sure, a super-smart race can build ships to cross oceans of space, but when they get here, what will they really know about us? I'm thinking nothing. Squat.

"I mean, when they get here and look through their super telescopes at us, maybe they'll see a human out walking a dog and believe it's the dog who is the master, leading a slave on a leash. Right?

"So, what will these aliens do? They'll send down a scout team, right? And this scout team? They don't know nothin'. I'll give them the ability to blend in by looking like humans and maybe have a secret language translator buried in their ears, but our customs and way we do things? Squat.

"Take dressing. They'll look around at all the different styles of clothes — like your clothes, old man clothes, or the clothes of cool dudes like me, and they'll come up with something. But, it will be wrong. Like the women on the team will only cover one breast and leave the other out."

Yeah, high school male. Jake expected Levi could see the cover of his book in his mind now: A sexy warrior woman with only one breast covered, death rays zapping around, and maybe a green alien reptile hissing in the background.

"I call my book, *The Bungled Invasion of Earth*. What do you think? Want the first crack at it?"

Jake paused, searching for words. "Different is great in publishing. Who would have thought vampires living up the road in Forks, dating ordinary teenage girls, would be publishing gold? But that's precisely what happened with the Twilight saga.

"And *The Bungled Invasion of Earth* is a catchy name. I'd certainly look twice if I were to see that book title. But, you might do best by searching for a specialty publisher, some company that knows how to market to the sci-fi community. Or, publish yourself on Amazon. They make it easy and have tons of readers in niche categories."

Disappointment flashed across Levi's face but didn't stick around.

"OK, bro. Thanks for the advice. And remember, I gave you the first shot. Maybe you are right: This idea is too big for anyone in this town. We can part as friends, though, right?" Levi stuck out his hand for Jake to shake.

Jake watched Levi thread his way between desks to the door and wondered if the kid would ever get his book published and, if he did, if Jake would be "one of the many" who rejected his idea before it hit big. Maybe it was Jake who didn't know squat.

"Bing's Bitches is taking off," said Bing, charging towards Jake from across the room. "We've already gotten five calls. Well, one was pretty obscene, but the others were gold. I should be able to fill half a page in this week's edition, especially when I add a couple of my own.

"That'll be good for you," she continued, "because I haven't seen John around, and Pat's been on the phone with her daughter all morning. Am I the only one who works around here?"

Drawing himself away from thoughts of half-naked women invaders and back into the newspaper world, Jake asked: "What have the calls been about?"

"One was about the rain like somebody would complain about that? Two others were about annoying neighbors with barking dogs. But the best one — maybe you should look into it — the caller spoke secretly low on the phone, saying his neighbor was up to something no good.

"Two or three times a month, cars from out the area — and he knew they were from out of the area because of the ads on the license plate holders — would park all around the almost deserted warehouse at the port district. He watched workers take in TV equipment, like cameras and lights, and people quickly hustled into the building. He thinks someone is filming porn movies there.

"These neighbors moved in a few months ago from out of town. They're living on the second floor of the port building and filming on the lower floor."

Bing looked down with a disdainful grimace. "This was another dumb idea by the port — they built these industrial buildings out on the edge of town, hoping to bring in high-tech manufacturers. Like high-tech people are going to move here. I guess the port is letting people live in the buildings now.

"Anyway, out-of-towners, secret filming, maybe porn. What a start to Bing's Bitches!"

Jake froze. He knew the idea for this column was so wrong, and now the proof was coming in. Unproven assertions of a porn movie operation. Yet… yet… it would be readers' gold. Probably the best-read item in the paper.

"Write it up. Let me take a look."

"Write it up? I already told you that the iPhone writes it up by transcribing the calls. I've already sent it to you. You know, for an editor, you are behind the times. You should pay attention more to what is going on around you."

CHAPTER 15

"Hey, I've got something for you on those bodies in the freezers."

Sheriff Ramblewood had called Jake early Tuesday morning, likely knowing he'd appreciate hot news the day before publication.

"That meeting I had to leave for yesterday was with the State Patrol. They have tracked down information on the RV."

Jake twisted his neck to cradle the phone while calling up a new screen on his computer. "Who owns it?"

"That, they don't know. But they did talk to the previous owner. Some old guy just a couple of miles out of Napavine."

"Napa? The bodies are from California?"

"Not Napa, Napavine, a little town halfway between Seattle and Portland off I-5. The man told the State Patrol he lives on a rural road out of town and had the toy hauler parked in his yard for sale for some time. He had about given up on selling it when some guy came to the door. The original price was $5,000, but when the guy took out a wad of hundreds and offered $3,000, the old guy took it."

"Is there a name for the buyer? Something on a bill of sale?"

"Nope. The buyer didn't say who he was, he just took the title the seller signed and drove off.

"The odd thing was, said the seller, he lives on a narrow country road. He didn't see any vehicle that could have brought the buyer to his house and had never seen the buyer before. The guy walked up, fished out $3,000 in hundreds, and drove off in the rig.

"All he asked, said the seller, was if the rig ran. When the seller said it did, the buyer started it up, seemed satisfied, and left."

"That all sounds strange."

"One more thing. The State Patrol, in closely examining the wrecked RV, saw the tires were 15 years old. You should replace tires every five years on RVs, even if the tread is good. The front right tire blew out, likely causing the RV to veer off the road suddenly.

"When the State Patrol returned to the seller, he said, 'The buyer never asked about the tires, so I never told him.' Nice guy, huh?"

*****

The murder of the cranberry grower dominated the front page, along with a feature sidebar about Darrell Green, his family, and their deep roots in the community. Everyone had nice things to say about what a wonderful, generous guy he was.

Except for the son, Bobby, who never returned calls from the paper.

The update on the RV and its cargo of bodies made a solid second story on the page. None of the bodies were those of local people, which further added to the mystery.

Jake didn't need — and didn't have room for — a third story, but where was John and his talking dolphin story anyway? One more week of no stories, Jake may have to let John go — a heritage employee or not.

"Jake, John's on one for you." Bing waved her phone around.

"John, where have you been?"

"Shhhh… I'm flying low these days, trying to keep out of sight. Next week, though, I break the big one."

"John, there's a difference between flying low and not flying at all. We'll have to have a conversation when this issue is out. Pat and I can't fill up the paper ourselves. You're getting to an age where you may not want to run down stories each week. Reporting for a weekly is hard work... barely time to catch your breath."

"Don't throw me overboard yet, boss. I'll have a knock-your-socks story next week. You can count on me. Yes sir. But, oops, now I have to go. I see my man."

Jake hung up, thinking he should call the newspaper broker, Dave Raymond, to see if he had the authority to fire an employee.

CHAPTER 16

"Hey, Bing, is there a check for me?"

It was draw day — the 15th of the month — and Jake looked up from laying out the sports section to see Bing handing Brandi and Adele their pay envelopes.

"No one told me to write you a check. Maybe you are still on a trial period."

A sound of exasperation blew past Jake's lips. "I dropped everything to come here," and then to himself, muttered, "If anything, I'm still trying out the newspaper. And unlike those fired CEOs who get a 'golden parachute' for leaving, I should be paid a 'golden parachute' for jumping in, rather than jumping out."

To Bing, he said, "Who tells you the amounts to pay each employee?"

"No one. I just paid everyone their regular salary. I paid Adele what she was paid before she retired. I held back John's check because I'm not sure he is actually *working* here ... and I gave myself a bump because of the extra effort with Bing's Bitches."

Jake went back to trying to write a gentle headline over the story for the girls' softball team that was swept in two games the past week. Looking at the lopsided scores, he couldn't use verbs like "nipped," "edged," or even "fell short." Being winless for the season was bad enough. These kids didn't need the local newspaper slamming them. Although "slamming" was a good softball headline verb, just not for this story.

"Jake, can I talk to you for a few minutes?"

"Sure, Pat, we are on a deadline here, though. What's

up?"

"I need to take a little time off."

"Like the rest of the day? You have your stories in, right? Take off today, and tomorrow, too?" Reporters mostly wasted time on press day anyway, drinking coffee and yakking in the office while the newspapers were printed and delivered. Giving her the rest of Tuesday and Wednesday off wouldn't hurt the story flow for next week.

"Probably the rest of this week." As usual, Pat sat on the extra chair by Jake's desk and stared past him out the window.

"It's my daughter. Ever since she turned 14, she has been a different person. We used to be 'mom-and-daughter this' and 'mom-and-daughter that,' baking cookies, solving Sudoku puzzles, going to yard sales, and then making fun of the junk people were trying to sell. We were a real team.

"It's like she went up to her room one day and then came down with a demon in her brain. Now, we fight all the time. It's been two years of hell. I am constantly grounding her. I caught her sneaking back into the house the night we were at the fire... she had snuck out earlier, and I didn't know.

"Seeing her come in way beyond midnight, I went ballistic. And, I'm sorry to say, when she sassed me back, I slapped her. I shouldn't have slapped her, and certainly not as hard as I did."

Having no children himself, Jake had nothing to offer. He had learned from conversations like this with other parents that the best approach was to say nothing. That's just what he did.

"She boarded a Greyhound the other day to Seattle — when she was supposed to go to school — then caught a transfer to Yakima, where her Dad lives.

"At least she left a note, so I didn't go nuts with worry, like the Beast Man got her. She called yesterday to say she would stay with him for a while. 'It's dry over here,' she said as if that were a reason.

"I will have to go to Yakima and work this out. I have full

custody, but he's not a bad guy when he's not drinking."

"OK." Jake had also learned long ago not to fight the inevitable regarding employees and their families. But he also liked to suggest some boundaries. "You think you can be back Monday, one way or another?"

"I hope to be back before then. Yakima is not my favorite city. Hills are too brown."

Jake returned to writing sports headlines. The high school student who covered sports for the paper had an excellent interview with the track coach. Maybe "Going the distance" could be a pun fun top headline with a subhead of "Coach optimistic for school runners this year."

"Jake, Scottie just called from the school," announced Bing, putting down her phone. "You know that interview he did with the track coach? He said you would have to pull it. The coach has been arrested for the murder of that cranberry grower, Darrell Green."

CHAPTER 17

"You arrested the track coach for killing your uncle? What was his reason?" Jake had phoned the sheriff immediately upon hearing of the arrest.

"I can't release any information right now. Tomorrow I'll talk with the media."

"We print this week's edition at 9 a.m. in Vancouver tomorrow. We cannot get the news into this week's paper if you don't talk with me today."

"I can't play favorites, Jake. Sorry. No favors."

"Sheriff, that's precisely what you are doing. By the time our edition hits local homes, everybody will have heard the news on their radio or from the regional daily newspapers. You are giving them an advantage over us, your hometown newspaper.

"Look, sheriff. I'm scrambling to rebuild the front page I have already laid out. I don't need an entire press release. I just need confirmation of what everyone at the school already knows, that the coach has been arrested. And then, one or two sentences from you about how your dogged investigation led to him."

"Dogged, huh? OK, but don't quote me directly. Or the other media will be all over me.

"It's true; we have arrested Bill Kelly, the track and basketball coach at the Long Beach High School. He is pending charges — not charged yet — in the death of cranberry grower Darrell Green. I won't say what evidence we have, but Green and Kelly have had business dealings in the past, and there may have been a falling out caused by a loss of money. And then, there is a belief by Kelly that Green was having an affair with his wife.

"That's it, Jake. No more. Do not put my name in the story. Not anywhere. Say sources at the sheriff's office or some such. Are we clear?"

"Yes, and thanks, sheriff, whose name I have already forgotten. I owe you one."

*****

Velma pushed the Mac & Jack's across the wooden bar to Jake. "That's $4."

"Four dollars? Usually, it's $5. What's this, happy hour?" he asked, looking around for a happy hour sign.

"Four dollars is the price for regulars."

"I'm regular now?"

"I don't know how regular you are, but you come in quite a bit. That qualifies you for the regulars price. I still expect a dollar tip with each beer, though. You're not regular enough to stop tipping me."

Jake laid a $5 bill on the bar, looked at the foaming head on the dark amber beer, and thought what a kaleidoscope life being a newspaperman was.

What a day! From getting an update on the frozen bodies case — where a nefarious scheme had crashed because of outdated tires on an RV — to hearing of a mother's worries over a runaway child and then tearing up the front page because of a cranberry grower couldn't keep it in his pants.

And now, regular pricing at the Green Hornet. How sweet it is!

"Enjoy it now because life as you know it is about to end."

"Oh, hi, John. I didn't realize I spoke out loud. What are you saying?"

John drew in a long breath and followed with a heavy exhale. "Jake, how much do you know about the history of bootlegging and smuggling?"

"I was a journalism major, John, so I wouldn't have to

read dry history books."

"Then it's going to take a while to explain. Maybe I should have something to keep my throat lubricated."

Jake looked up to catch Velma's eye, but she was already pouring. "Do I get regular pricing on his drinks, too?"

"Oh, he's a regular, that's for sure." She pushed a golden drink over ice cubes to John.

John raised the glass to his lips, closed his eyes, and took a sip. What happened next was like watching a movie in slow motion: Jake could see John's facial features relax as the drink ran over the front of his tongue, then his head and shoulders moved back as the liquid flowed to the base of the tongue and then down the throat. Tension oozed out of John's body, his shoulders drooped, and his back curved into the bar. Finally, the alcohol hit John's bloodstream. His eyes popped open to a clear new world. He was ready to talk.

"You know we had Prohibition in the 1920s and 1930s, where a decent working man couldn't get a little taste to ease the world's burdens, right?"

"Yeah, I saw the movies on Al Capone and Bugsy Moran."

"Movies, pffft." John eased another drink into his mouth. "Hollywood loves Chicago mobsters, machine guns, and bathtub hooch. But the real story was the smuggling of high-quality liquor from Canada into the U.S., and the best smugglers were right here along Washington's coast."

"OK. I didn't know that."

"The most famous of Washington smugglers was an ex-cop from Seattle named Roy Olmstead. He used speedy boats and clever routes through the San Juan islands to evade the Coast Guard. He was so famous he became known as the King of Puget Sound Bootleggers.

"But, being famous is not a good career move for a smuggler. And he was eventually taken down by the G-men."

John quietly drummed his fingers against his empty glass. Out came another $5 from Jake's wallet. Velma was already pouring.

"The smuggler that few people have heard of, and in my mind, the most successful West Coast bootlegger, was a Russian known as Big Red. And, he operated right out of Long Beach."

"Wow, really?" Jake looked up from watching John to see Velma standing nearby, thoroughly drying a glass with a towel. This struck Jake as odd, as she usually moved away from customers. She never seemed to be the friendly ear bartenders are known for.

"Big Red brought Canadian booze down in larger boats, then offloaded onto smaller speed boats that could land at inlets, harbors, and sloughs around here. Once on land, the liquor could be quickly transferred into trucks and shipped anywhere.

"Being Russian, Big Red distrusted government and authority. His gang was a tight-knit crew of Russians whose families had fled here when the Communists consolidated their hold on Russia. He controlled various homes, never sleeping in the same place — or with the same woman — for too long.

"He is reputed to have made a whale of a fortune that he stashed in places only he knew because, like most Russians, he was paranoid to a fault. And," John dropped his voice dramatically, "that fortune has never been found."

"Uh-uh. OK. But a fortune in those days was $20,000, $30,000? Not worth much today. That is if the horde of cash hasn't rotted away."

"Silver. Big Red loved silver. He wore one silver earring, like a pirate. He loved stories of pirates. And his nickname was honest. He was big and tough with flaming red hair. He could get away wearing whatever he wanted. He said the silver in the earring talked to him, telling him how to get more silver."

Jake laughed. "Oh, John, a swashbuckler named Big Red. You had us going, right Velma?"

She shook her head. "These stories have been whispered around for years."

Taking his last swallow, John stood up. "And now Russians have come to town, looking for Big Red's fortune.

"What do you mean?"

"We have Russian criminals here. I'm even wondering if the lure of the silver isn't the real reason the McKinneys bought the *Beachcomber*, to use the newspaper as a front as they asked questions and ran down leads around town."

"McKinneys? How would the McKinneys know about the fortune? McKinney is an Irish name, I believe."

"That was Miles' name. Jane was Russian, 100 percent Russian descent, with her blonde good looks and Russian love for money."

"Wow, that raises new questions about the McKinneys. But how does this affect me?

"The way you showed up suddenly to take over the paper, the people responsible for the deaths of the McKinneys might think you know something about the treasure. You could be next. Watch your back. And watch those closest to you." John's eyes swung over to Velma and, with a nod, was off into the rainy evening.

CHAPTER 18

Was that sunlight coming through the window? It was! Unbelievable.

Jake propped himself on one elbow to look at the poplar trees lining the *Beachcomber's* parking lot. It was actual sunshine sparkling off water drops on the new leaves.

Jake's movements woke Ruby. "Hey, it's too early to get up. Or do you have to get to work?"

"I'm taking a sunshine morning. Bing already thinks I'm a slacker, so that's what slackers do, right? Besides, she's still at the press, getting the papers printed."

Ruby propped herself up, too. "Wait, what's that big bright thing in the sky? I vaguely remember it, but I don't recall its name... starts with an 's'...."

Jake bent his head to kiss the back of Ruby's bare neck. "I am so happy you are here with me. Without you, I don't know if I could have put up with all the dismal days and nights."

"Jake, you're all right, too. Say, since I'm working and we're roomies, would you like me to pay for half of the expenses?"

"Pffft... there are very few expenses. I'm parking for free, a few bucks to keep the propane tank full, so we have hot meals and showers, food, and a couple of bottles of wine a week is about all I spend money on. Not enough that in good conscience, I could even make you 'work off' the expenses."

Ruby's face darkened. "That's not a joke I like, Jake."

"Sorry, sorry. Just trying to be funny. My error."

"And I'm sorry for saying anything. Most of the time, I love your sense of humor and how you keep everything light.

Life can be hard, so let's have all the fun we can along the way."

"Did I hear fun? How about this for a little fun?"

Ruby giggled.

Knocking erupted on the RV's door. "Mr. Editor man, Mr. Editor man! I gotta talk to you."

"Aargh, what terrible timing that woman has!" Jake jumped up and slid on jeans and a tee. This time, Ruby got up, too, and pulled on an oversized Seahawks jersey from Jake's closet.

"Mary Teresa," Jake said, swinging open the door, "what brings you out so early?"

"Early? It's not early, it's almost 9." She placed one foot on the bottom stair, pushed her body forward, and continued up as Jake backed off.

"Oh, hi Missy," she said, seeing Ruby, then noticed her preparing the Keurig, added, "Black for me. And I'm in a hurry, so make mine first."

"I'm also reheating leftover baked potatoes and air-fried steak from last night. Would you like some?" asked Ruby.

"I'm not hungry at all," said Mary Teresa, sliding into a bench seat. "No more than a third for me."

Jake pulled the cup of coffee from the Keurig and placed it before Mary Teresa. "What can I do for you?"

"Well… do you have some ketchup to go with that steak? Reheated food can get so dry. Maybe some horseradish, too? Give it a little kick."

Jake rummaged through the fridge, pulled out a couple of plastic containers, and placed them on a mat on the table. "Again, you wanted to talk?"

"Yes, oh, thanks, Missy." Mary Teresa stabbed a steak bite from the plate Ruby served, chewed, and then looked up. "My coffee is gone. One more cup before I leave. Make it easy on yourself, Missy, just black."

Ruby turned around to the Keurig on the kitchen counter, her stomach heaving as she suppressed a laugh.

"Mary Teresa, I have to get to work soon."

"Yes, I just wanted to take a minute to thank you for getting the sheriff off the backs of the vets. I hear you really went to bat for them. You're doing an OK job at the newspaper, I don't care what Bing says."

The comment about Bing annoyed Jake, but the praise about the vets surprised him, as he had said little to the sheriff. Still, never argue with a compliment was his rule.

Jake saw Ruby holding back serving their breakfast until Mary Teresa left. "I see you're about finished. Don't let us hold you up. We must take a few quick showers and be off ourselves."

"Of course. As my Dad used to say, 'An honest day's pay for an honest day's work.' I don't want to hold you up from getting that day started. Better late than never."

Mary Teresa started to rise, then sat back down. "Oh, one more thing. I told you I make coffee for some homeless vets who pass at the back of my land to and from their camps in the woods. I often stand out there and talk with them. Their stories are fascinating. But also, there is a very active grapevine among these guys. And some women, too. There are homeless women vets out there, too — damn shame.

"Anyway, these guys — and women — make a point of not standing out, or else they will be rousted from parks, benches, the beach. By blending into the background, they see and hear a lot. And that information gets passed around."

"OK, like anything special?"

"Yeah. That track coach? He didn't kill the cranberry grower."

CHAPTER 19

Jake was in the office when Bing returned with the freshly printed papers. With the rushed activity of getting the papers ready for delivery, he didn't notice she was avoiding him.

An hour later or so, however, he realized she hadn't said a word to him all morning. He thought she would be all over him, crowing about her column, Bing's Bitches, complaining about John's work habits — or non-work habits — or asking if Pat should be docked a couple of days' pay for leaving town to check on her daughter.

"Bing, I talked with your sister this morning. She is happy the homeless vets she works with are off the radar in the murder of the cranberry grower."

When those words didn't generate a response, Jake asked: "Is everything all right? You seem unusually quiet this morning."

She swiveled in her chair towards Jake. "I am so excited about my column, the first thing I do every morning is check for messages. I even checked this morning before leaving for the press, though nothing from last night couldn't get into this week's edition."

She paused, then added: "There's a message you should listen to."

She hit "play" on the answering machine, and a gruff voice came on.

"You tell that editor of yours he either returns my Jessie and what she owes me, or I'll burn that heap of an RV with him in it. You tell him I'm coming for him and won't leave until I get satisfaction."

The room went quiet momentarily, the threat hovering in the air.

"Obviously, Jake, I'm not going to put that call into next week's column — although it would be gold — but who is Jessie, where did you take her from, and what will you do?"

"It's a long story, Bing. Let me think about it. Maybe I should talk with Sheriff Ramblewood." But first, he thought, he needed to speak with Ruby.

"Well, I wouldn't want what happened to the McKinneys to happen to you. They were no great shakes as newspaper operators either, but I liked their two little boys."

"What do you mean... 'what happened to the McKinneys'?"

"Well, they call it an accident, but it was no accident." Bing wheeled her chair over to Jake's desk, having recovered her mojo.

"The McKinneys went to Astoria, across the bridge into Oregon, on a date night after putting the newspaper out on Wednesday. I would think after two kids, and ten years of marriage, they would be beyond dating. But anyway, on the way back — Miles was at the wheel, probably drunk as he was a drinker, like you — when they came out of the tunnel just this side of the bridge. That's where it gets strange.

"It's a straight road there, but at first, it looked like Mile's just steered off the road for no reason, striking a huge maple tree. There were no skid marks, no tire marks at all, just like he turned into the tree.

"Both he and Jane were killed instantly. He must have been going fast, probably hurrying to get home and save a few bucks on the babysitter. He was rather tight. Never gave me a raise in all the time they were here."

She scooted her chair closer to Jake. "The county mounties responded to the crash, and all that night and the following day, they considered it a one-car accident. They are not all that competent. I know, my sister is one of them. Anyway, it wasn't until kids playing in the woods spotted a wrecked motorcycle with a dead rider that questions started being asked.

"Wait, your sister, Mary Teresa, is a deputy?"

"No, dummy, who said that? My other sister, Mary Grace, she's the county mountie. Fits her personality to a T — she loves to lord it over you."

"OK, so this is the first time I've heard there was a motorcycle involved. Sheriff Ramblewood did say the accident was baffling. What do you suppose she meant?"

"Well..."

"Stop the presses, young man, I got a front-page story for you!" John Ryan burst into the newsroom, waving a worn reporter's notebook, a pleased smile on his face.

"John, the press for this week's edition ran this morning. What are you talking about?"

"Ha, I just love saying that. Said it a few times in my life, too. I've probably stopped more presses than any reporter alive."

John rolled his chair over to join Bing and Jake. "Stopped many a press run to get a killer story in print... although to be fair, editors have stopped the presses a few times to get one of my stories off, too, when some key fact turned out to be not quite totally true — or they were worried about libel. Editors are a scared bunch."

"You have the talking dolphin story, at last, I take it?"

"Nah, that's a wonderful, feel-good story that will go national after it's in the *Beachcomber*. You'll be on TV talking about how the newspaper got that story. Not me," he grinned towards Bing, "I've got a face made for newspaper work.

"Nope. Here's the hammer headline at the top of next week's *Beachcomber*." He spread his hands through the air as if seeing a theater marquee: 'Moroccan Law invasion!'"

CHAPTER 20

Moroccan Law?

What is it with this small-town newspaper, wondered Jake. How does the news get so weird? Bodies in freezers slung around the highway, mysterious deaths of the newspaper's owners, rustlers in the cranberry bogs — a story he hadn't yet had time to run down — killer fog, a Beast Man running amok in the woods, homeless vets ghosting through town, a dolphin who talks…

No wonder he approved Bing's Bitches. In comparison, an anonymous gossip column seems a reasonably tame idea.

"Jake, I can tell by your stunned silence just how earth-shaking you think this story is. And," John turned to grin again at Bing, who was stunned into silence for once, "I can tell you are wondering if I'll be able to nail down the story by next week's deadline.

"I'll be honest with you, Jake, I'll need help. There are many avenues to explore, so much research to be done, so many people to talk to, and so many facts to weave together into a seamless flowing epic. I don't think one man can do it all, not even me.

"Got your truck here? Grab your notebook, and let's go for a ride. Oh, maybe a quick stop at the Green Hornet for lunch on the *Beachcomber*, and then once more unto the breach, dear friends."

"John, quoting Shakespeare doesn't get you a free lunch, but yeah, OK. I think I deserve something for the morning I've had too."

*****

John was uncharacteristically quiet on the drive to the Green Hornet, fidgeting on the pickup's bench seat, now and then looking skyward as though he couldn't believe the gray clouds had peeled away to reveal blue.

Even a honey-colored drink failed to loosen his lips. "Just two for me," John said when the first was gone before the food order arrived. "This story is going to take all my concentration."

After lunch, in the pickup heading north of town on Highway 103, John closely watched the driveways and houses built along the ocean. Long Beach was famous for its extensive sandy beach — at 28 miles, the Long Beach peninsula was the longest continuous beach in the U.S. Over the decades, lovely homes had sprung up to capture the ocean view.

"There, right there, the one with the mermaid carving. Turn in that driveway."

Jake waited for an older blue Volkswagen van — surfboards roped to the side, a surfer dude, blond curls spilling out of a stocking cap at the wheel — to pass, then turned left. He was immediately stopped by deck chairs blockading the driveway.

A bed sheet spread between two volleyball poles proclaimed in red paint lettering: "Seized under Moorish Law."

"What the hell?"

"Jake, I downloaded a clipping from The Herald in Everett. I'll save my breath and let it give you the background."

Jake opened the folded sheet of paper from John and began to read.

EDMONDS — Two members of a sovereign citizen group broke into a vacant $4.5 million home in Woodway, claiming they had seized the property under Moorish law, according to police.

Six times since October, residents of Edmonds or Woodway have reported self-proclaimed Moorish sovereigns showing up to expensive homes uninvited and claiming the legal right to seize the property. Many adherents of the extremist movement claim they are exempt from all civil or criminal law, citing a fictitious treaty from 1787, according to the Southern Poverty Law Center.

One of the men, 46, of Mountlake Terrace, is listed as part of the Supreme Judiciary of a group known as the Moorish National Republic Federal Government.

"The suspects had posted a notice on the property's for sale sign indicating their new ownership under Moroccan Law," police said.

"Jake, I have another clipping from New Jersey where a group with a similar name took over a woman's home. Men broke in, changed her locks, and hung a red and green flag in a window. They claimed they were sovereign citizens of a different country for whom United States laws do not apply.

"The woman called the police, but it took a SWAT team showing up to get the men out.

"And even then, she kept getting letters on official-looking letterhead from something called the Al Moroccan Empire saying she was not the house's valid owner.

"Jake, I think we have an outbreak of Moroccan Law here."

CHAPTER 21

"We are the legal owners of this fine house. That is my name on the deed."

The man in the red fez held a document with several signatures, a notary stamp, and a flourish of an official-looking logo across the top. "That's the Al Moroccan seal," explained the man, "making this all legal."

Another man and woman stood beyond him in the doorway, nodding their heads when the man in the red fez talked. He had come to the door when Jake and John knocked and only agreed to speak to them once they identified themselves as reporters with the local newspaper.

"We have had trouble with police in the past not recognizing our rights," said the man, who didn't want to give his name.

"Help me understand," Jake empathized, "you didn't pay for this house, you didn't buy it from the previous owners. How can you come into a house not listed as yours on county records and take it?"

"We all here are sovereign citizens of the Al Moroccan Empire. We people who are Moorish sovereign citizens are bound by maritime law, not the law of this country."

Along with his red fez topped with a tassel that bounced when he spoke, the man wore a tan suit, white shirt, red tie, and black dress shoes. He was tall and athletic-looking, and his soft, rich voice was reasonable as he addressed Jake and John.

"Look, you probably know a little maritime law from working here along the ocean. And one of the tenets of maritime law is that a ship abandoned at sea is open game... anyone can come along and claim it. That's why big companies, when one of their freighters gets in trouble at sea, leave at least one crew member on board so someone like me can't come along and claim it."

Jake vaguely recalled hearing about such a law of the sea but couldn't say whether it was true or a myth. It kind of seemed reasonable. He certainly remembered stories of ships breaking apart near the coast, and when their cargo washed ashore, it was available for public picking.

"So, for us," continued the man, "it works the same on land. This house has no one in it. To us, driving down the highway, it looks abandoned. No lights were on, no cars in the driveway, and all the curtains were pulled. When we knocked on the doors, no one answered. So, by our laws, maritime law, we claimed the house. We went through the process, and now we have the Moorish deed — to the house.

"Done and settled."

"You don't look Moroccan, and I don't believe foreign laws apply in the U.S.," replied Jake.

A smile spread on the man's face as though looking at a petulant child. "Have you ever been to Morocco to know what Moroccans look like?"

"No..."

"I thought not. You don't look like an international citizen." He laughed, "See, I don't know anything about you, and I made a biased judgment about you, just like you made a subjective judgment about me, although you only met me a few moments ago.

"Now, my friend, the law is a complicated animal. Any law in any country. It turns out — and I myself didn't know this until a few years ago — long ago, in the 1800s or before, the United States and Morocco signed a treaty to honor each other's laws in their native countries. That means if you *were* to travel to Morocco and commit some offense, like insulting Allah, you couldn't be lashed publicly by a holy man.

"Conversely..." the man spread his large hands, "this

house is now ours.

     "Good day, gentlemen. It's time for afternoon prayers."

CHAPTER 22

"Jake, do you believe in reincarnation?" asked Ruby.

"Reincarnation? I haven't thought much about what happens after I die, but..." he gestured towards the answering machine on Bing's desk. He had brought Ruby to the office after work Wednesday to hear the message from the angry man demanding Jessie back.

"I don't mean reincarnation like the Hindus believe, where you come back as a bug or a better human, depending on how good you were in a past life. No, when I think of reincarnation, I think it's possible to live many lives in the one life you are given.

"Ten minutes before you met me at the gas station, I was living one life. Five minutes after I climbed into your RV, I was living a different life. Maybe the goodness or badness of the previous life — what I was living 10 minutes before — didn't determine my new life, but what I learned in the past life helped me choose a new, better life."

"Sure, people can change, and their lives can change. A few weeks ago, I was sitting in a bar in sunny Yuma with a Jailbait Blonde...."

"Stop, Jake. This isn't about you.

"You might think a woman's life is easy — equal pay, equal rights, all that. But a woman's life is not easy. This is still a man's world; a woman can find herself at the beck and call of a truly unpleasant man. But if she works hard enough, has enough imagination, enough nerve, she can reinvent herself — reincarnate herself — into a new life of her own making."

"Yeah, OK. But still, this phone call...."

"Ignore it. That's what I'm choosing to do."

"Look, Ruby, I've been asleep in an RV when an insane ex-husband set it on fire, and it's not something I want to go through again. I think we should go to the police, but first, I want to understand what is happening. What kind of life did you lead before you were 'reincarnated'?"

Ruby's face turned dark. She looked for several seconds at him. "I'm enjoying my time with you, Jake, you're cute and fun. But I could reincarnate myself right into a new life if you don't leave my past alone."

She turned, walked out the door, paused momentarily, chose not to walk to the RV, and turned towards the beach.

*****

With Ruby angry with him, it was time to see the Green Hornet.

"Velma, what is the story about the bee in the box anyway?"

The barmaid laid a fresh Indian Pale Ale called Moving Day from Wet Coast Brewery in front of Jake. He had picked the beer off the chalkboard menu, thinking the name might suggest something.

"Him?" she nodded at the full-sized mannequin in a green bee suit enclosed in the acrylic display case on the back bar.

"Well, yeah, like there is any other buzz-man in a box around. People must ask you about that all the time. There's got to be an interesting backstory."

"Not so much. Four dollars."

"Regulars' price, right? Come on, tell me the story."

Velma folded her hands and placed them on the bar as she leaned toward Jake.

"Well... " then, looking past Jake, hollered out, "Hey you, we don't want you in here!" She waved a finger towards the door, pointing the way out for a tall figure who had just come in.

Jake turned abruptly, saw a man in a green coat and fatigues, and said to Velma, "You don't allow veterans in here?"

"Veterans? I'm a vet. We love veterans. But these homeless guys who wander through town, either come in here, spend all their monthly disability checks on beer, get drunk, and cause fights, or order one coffee and sit in the corner all day out of the rain. Either way, they're not good for business."

Jake realized he recognized the vet. He was the guy on the street corner who said "Larry" hadn't meant to attack Jake at the cranberry bog.

And now, although not looking directly at Jake, he seemed to give an almost imperceptible nod toward the outside before pushing out the door.

"I better go check this out," said Jake, rising from his stool. "Can you save this for me?"

"We're not the Salvation Army, there is no saving here. Drink it or lose it if you leave."

Torn between a cold beer after a grueling day or a possible story, Jake took a long swallow, emptying half the glass. Ugh, craft beers were not made for chugging.

Exiting the front door, Jake looked left then right, seeing the vet posted up by the bus stop shelter.

"Sarge says you're all right," he said when Jake approached. "She says we can talk to you."

"Uh, sure. What's up?"

"Larry didn't see the murder at the cranberry bog."

"OK..."

"But he knows who did."

"Wait, someone saw the murder? Has he talked with the sheriff?"

The tall man stared off at a passing logging truck. When the roar from the diesel engine died down, he continued. "She doesn't like to leave the woods. Says it's not safe."

"Her? OK. How did she see the murder if she didn't leave camp?"

"The old cranberry man was nice to her and gave her

food sometimes. Listened when she talked. Didn't ask for…" and the burly stranger looked Jake directly in the eye for the first time, "… you know."

Jake could well guess what the vet was implying between an older man and a vulnerable younger woman. He continued with his questions. "She was there when he was murdered? Did she do it?"

"Not her!" He shook his head angrily at Jake. "She was coming for food when she saw him get hit."

"Who hit him?"

"Larry doesn't know. She hasn't told him."

As he had begun to suspect, Jake realized the man talking was Larry himself.

"Maybe Larry should talk to the sheriff and share this story. The wrong man has been arrested."

"No."

"OK. How about if Larry takes me to the woman who saw the murder? I can talk to her, hear the details and then talk myself to the sheriff," and get a front-page story for next week's *Beachcomber*, thought Jake.

"Maybe," the man said, then drifted down the street.

*****

When Ruby returned to the RV later Wednesday evening — and in a friendly mood — Jake was surprised by how relieved he was.

Jake had had many girlfriends and even a wife, but he never entirely caught on to how women think or, more importantly, how they think about him.

But he had learned one lesson — if a woman walks away and returns, she had probably carefully weighed the benefits and drawbacks of a relationship and decided she was better off with him than without him. A woman who came back was more committed to the relationship than ever.

And a second lesson was not to screw it up. Don't be

mad, don't double down on the behavior that drove her away in the first place, and don't ask questions. Just thank your lucky stars and welcome her home.

And Jake did welcome her, more than once, Wednesday night.

*****

An elbow in the ribs woke Jake.

"Jake, I can't sleep. Tell me more about Big Red and his fortune. I like to hear the sound of your voice."

"You mean my voice will put you to sleep?"

"No, no, your story will give me something new to think about, get my mind off the track it's on now, keeping me awake."

"OK. That's a nice way of saying the same thing. I don't know much more. John Ryan did imply there is a horde of silver somewhere around, and now dangerous people are looking for it.

"But honestly, I always doubted stories of gangsters' treasure troves and pirates' buried booty. It never seemed to me that gangsters or pirates were the types to be putting away a little something today for their retirement years. They always struck me as the kind of guys who spent everything they had today on wine and women because they were convinced they could steal more tomorrow."

"Yeah, but did John say what happened to Big Red?"

"No, as a matter of fact, he didn't. Maybe I'll look in the archives of the *Beachcomber* tomorrow. Maybe I can find an obit or a story on his arrest."

"What if he just disappeared? Maybe he wouldn't have had a chance to spend his smuggling profits?"

"Yeah, maybe. Now you have me awake. I wonder..."

"Let's leave that wondering 'til morning because now I'm wondering if Jane McKinney left any notes about the treasure and how you could find those notes. Let your mind wonder about that. I'll be here in the morning."

Jake turned back over to wonder about the treasure. And as he did, a quiet question seeped into his brain: Why was Ruby so interested?

CHAPTER 23

When Jake came to work Thursday morning, he saw a sight he had never seen at the *Beachcomber*: John Ryan at his desk, punching out a story.

"Punching" was the correct verb, as John was typing furiously, using only the pointer fingers on each hand, stabbing letters on the computer keyboard.

Jake stood silently for a few minutes at the front counter, watching John moving his lips, mouthing the story as he typed, grinning as if laughing at a private joke every so often.

Jake quietly walked to his desk to avoid disturbing the determined reporter, then started creating a story list for next week's paper.

John's story on the man who claimed the unoccupied home along the beach in the name of Moroccan Law would be on page one. A background story pulling together similar incidents around the country could go on page three. The news story — such as if the sheriff was going to roust out the Moors — would have to be done Tuesday, on deadline. John could probably do that story, too.

Jake had other mysteries to solve.

While the high school coach had been arrested in the murder of the cranberry grower, the prosecutor hadn't charged him. Jake planned to track down the apparently only witness to the crime and get an interview. That story would also go on page one.

And then there were the strange surroundings around the deaths of the McKinneys, the paper's former owners. And what was happening to their sons, a question he was often asked by local people when Jake ventured out. A lovely story about the boys would be well read. That could be a story for Pat, when and if the reporter returned from reuniting with her daughter.

And there were personal mysteries to solve. While he wouldn't repeat the mistake of asking Ruby about her past, the threatening message on the answering machine couldn't be ignored. He needed to talk to the sheriff, and soon.

Then, what was to come of the *Beachcomber*? At some quiet moment in the office, Jake needed to make another call to Dave Raymond and light a fire under the newspaper broker.

Well... on second thought, maybe no need for haste.

Now that the sun had shown its face, Jake was taking a brighter view of the town where he was working and realized — once again — how much he enjoyed the odd characters around a newspaper.

He was reminded of a joke a small city mayor once told him about picking a political party to belong to.

"I was in college, thinking about running for office one day, and decided to get involved with a political party. Growing up, my family had no real affiliations, so I thought I would check both of them out.

"The first one I went to was the Young Republicans. Very respectable, many dressed in suits, the meeting ran on an agenda with Robert's Rules of Order closely followed.

"Next, I went to the Young Democrats. Free beer, lots of shouting, and then a fight broke out. I decided right there, *this* is the party for me!"

In the past year and a half, Jake had discovered he was a little like that mayor. In his career at the Seattle *Times*, the dignified but stodgy paper was the Republicans in the mayor's joke. Half of the reporters still wore ties to work, as most of the editors did, and usually, all the actors in the big stories played roles, cued along by their media relations experts.

But at the two weeklies, he worked at — first in Arizona and now here — the people at the papers and those who made the news came with a full range of human eccentricities.

Humans were complex, confusing, and contrary animals. At big-city newspapers, humans were molded into "types" with any nonconforming characteristics trimmed away at the editing desk. The irony of community newspapers was though rural areas were considerably more conservative than metro areas, people in small towns were more willing to let their "freak flags" fly.

It made every day a new adventure for a newsman with open eyes like Jake.

*****

"What if there were a pandemic and everyone lost all their teeth? Imagine an entire world of people without teeth. Healthy otherwise, but without teeth.

"They tried dentures, but changes in the jaw bone structure made them uncomfortable.

"Imagine how that one fact would change so much. All the industries supplying foods we need teeth for would be bankrupted... no more beef steaks, no popcorn, no English muffins, no pizza.

"Imagine, no need for dentists or toothbrush manufacturers."

Jake let Levi pitch his latest idea for a sci-fi book. Or it could be a horror story. Jake had more than once had nightmares about losing his teeth. Dream analysis said it was a fear of getting old. Jake wasn't afraid of getting old, but he cringed, remembering dreams of his teeth falling out.

"Levi, that's an intriguing idea. Great concept for a book. It could be a best seller. Maybe even a movie. But again, I say, we don't publish sci-fi."

Jake looked past the high school-aged one-named author towards the office manager. "Bing, what's that book you are getting ready to send to the printers next week?"

"*How to Identify Freaky Fungi in the Fringy Forests*. It's written by a microbiologist at the University of Washington.

There are many color photos and not too much of his blah, blah, blah. I edited out everything that bored me," replied Bing. "Maybe I could look at the kid's book and help him cut out the dull parts."

Levi didn't rise to the jibe from Bing. Instead, he leaned in closer to Jake. "Listen, I'm trying to help you out here. Everybody knows these little newspapers are in pain and dying. You need to pivot to a new profit model. There is no future in cheap ink printed on dead trees."

"Cheap ink on printed dead trees? That's the definition of book publishing, isn't it?"

"I don't want you to *print* my book. What do you think I am asking, anyway? I don't want *printed* books. I want my books to be where the readers are, on their iPads and Kindles.

"Here's what I need. I'm a creative guy with great ideas and a flair for writing. But, what I am weak at — and any of my high school teachers would agree — is meeting deadlines.

"I need a demanding publisher to whip me over the finish line, take my creative genius, massage it, do the necessary editing, and then work the technical side to get my story online. And once published by Amazon and the other ebook publishers, promote the hell out of it to drive sales."

"I'm the talent. But talent is worthless, hidden in his mother's basement. Elvis would have been a nobody, never more than a truck driver, if Colonel Sanders hadn't gotten a hold of him. I want you to be my Colonel Sanders."

Jake shifted in his seat. "Tom Parker. Col. Tom Parker was the man who built up Elvis. Colonel Sanders fried chicken.

"But back to your book. Look, Levi, it's a very tempting offer for sure. But I think, for now, we'll stick with freaky fungi. Maybe we are too small time for your dreams."

Levi shook his head sadly, rose, and walked out. Jake noticed on his way past Bing's desk that she passed him a small piece of paper. I wonder what that was about, Jake mused, but his thoughts were interrupted by tapping on the window next to his desk.

CHAPTER 24

"You have shoes?"

"I have these." Jake raised one foot to show off his orange Nike sneakers. After the homeless vet knocked on the window, he went outside to talk with Larry.

"Better shoes. Hiking shoes. A grunt's shoes."

"Where am I going to be hiking?"

"To see Lanie. Get shoes at Goodwill today. Tomorrow. Oh nine hundred. Here. You can drive to the trailhead."

"Lanie is the woman who saw the murder of the cranberry grower?"

Larry nodded, turned, and walked down the street as silently as a deer fading into the brush.

*****

Luckily, the Goodwill in town did have a pair of size nine, well-broken-in hiking books to fit Jake's small feet. So, on Friday morning, he was standing beside his Tacoma pickup in a warm coat from Goodwill, covered by a rain slicker just in case and the new-to-him boots, when Larry appeared noiselessly beside him.

"Don't bring a gun."

"A gun? I don't have a gun. What would I need a gun for?"

"Lanie doesn't like men with guns. Or knives. Drive."

Guns and knives might be the tools of the trade for soldiers, but for Jake, the tools of the trade were a pen, reporter's notebook, and iPhone camera. Jake was coming well armed.

Once Larry had squeezed into the passenger side, Jake

felt the little pickup dip from the hefty vet's body. From a distance, the vet's gaunt face gave him a lean look, but up close, Larry was a big man, made bigger by the heavy camo coat and inseparable ruck pack.

After Larry ignored Jake's first couple of questions, the two men settled into an easy quiet, with Jake turning on the back roads when Larry nodded in one direction or another.

"Sarge's quarters." Larry shifted his eyes to a farmhouse they were passing. The house, set far from the road, was fronted by an overgrown hay field. A rusted tractor in the field had a large rear tire stuck in the mud. It looked like it got stuck quite a few years ago.

A large barn made of bare wood gone silver was within walking distance behind the house. Holes in the roof said the barn was little used these days. A pickup parked by the barn had grass two feet high growing from the bed.

"Here." Jake quickly braked and looked down a rutted road at the farm's property line. Probably a logging road left over from the days when the government habitually sold off timber — before the spotted owl environmental regulations came along.

Jake turned the control knob on the dash to the four-wheel-drive setting. It was the first time he had ever used the knob. He assumed it worked, and by the looks of the road, he would need traction from all four wheels to get through the muddy furrows plowed in the road by earlier traffic.

In a short distance of bouncing through the potholes — Jake was thankful he had the steering wheel to hold on to, while Larry grunted each time the pickup bottomed out — they came to a wide spot where a couple of full-sized American-made pickups were parked. Rusty and streaked with green algae, cracked windshields, and dented, these pickups were the old-timers of a harsh environment.

"Here."

Once parked, Jake saw a backyard canopy across the rough road, with a couple of men standing around Mary Teresa.

Each had a steaming cup of coffee and looked up at Jake and Larry as they crossed to the canopy.

"Hi, Editor man, going for a walk in the woods? You picked a good day for it," she said, looking towards a mist drifting in and out of the branches of the massive fir trees.

"Yes," said Jake, who owned a reporter's reluctance to share information about possible stories or sources, especially before they were talked to. "Larry offered to show me how the vets live in these woods.

Accepting a cup of brew from Mary Teresa, he asked, "So people can just live in these forests? That's OK with the government?"

"They are public forests, which means the public owns them. So yes, people can camp on public land. There are some rules. You should limit the camping to no more than two weeks, and you can't make any permanent change to the land."

"Oh, I thought some of these vets lived here semi-permanently."

"Yes, they do. Many of the people who work for the U.S. Forest Service were in the service themselves. They never seem to find the time to come out and run these vets out of their homes."

Jake turned to see Larry starting down a narrow trail into the trees. "Oh, I better go."

"Jake," Mary Teresa moved closer, "you want me to go fetch my granddad's shotgun if you run across the Beast?"

"Shotgun? No, no, I'll be fine with Larry."

He handed her the cup back, and as he turned away to follow Larry, he caught a fleeting glimpse of worry flying across Mary Teresa's face.

CHAPTER 25

Larry was a big man who took giant steps over a trail he knew well.

That wasn't the case with Jake, who had to scramble to keep up.

"Ouch! Damn it!" Jake was down for the third time, on his butt, rubbing a knee that collided with a tree trunk when he snagged a toe on an exposed root across the trail.

"What?" he responded to Larry's annoyed look. "Every time I look up to see where we're going, my foot slips or gets tripped up or steps into a hole. I'm not trying to hold us up."

Larry cast his eyes around. "Can't stop here."

Jake was about to ask why not when he heard a twig crack, followed by the racking of a pump-action shotgun being made ready to fire.

Jake grabbed Larry's offered hand, and the pair hustled down the hillside trail, Jake showing just how light he could be on his feet.

*****

"Lanie? Lanie? It's Larry."

Jake looked around at a clearing he hadn't seen before leaving the trail to follow Larry through heavy fir branches. Three majestic trees formed a triangle, their trunks thicker than round bar tables. Someone had carefully removed only the inner lower branches of the trees, leaving an open space roomier than his RV. It was carefully swept.

Clear sheet plastic woven between sweeping branches formed a ceiling that let in light but kept the space dry. A single bed was along one side, and two small wooden tables were along another side holding a plate, cup, and a single burner gas cooktop. A low flame was still dancing on the cooktop. Someone was nearby.

Larry and Jake stood on the third side, just outside the space covered by plastic, respecting the domain of the person who lived there.

The seconds passed, and then the minutes. Whoever said the woods were quiet had never been deep into the timber. Swaying branches from the gentle wind creaked overhead, birds called back and forth, and water gushed over rocks in a creek just beyond the three trees.

"Larry, who did you bring to my camp?"

Spooked by the voice, Jake jerked and turned to see a woman in her 30s, short black hair, a green tee stretched over a fit body, wearing fatigues and black lace-up boots. She was holding one hand behind her back. She wasn't offering a smiling welcome.

When Larry let the seconds pass without answering, Jake jumped in. "I'm the editor of the local newspaper. I'm doing a story on the murder of a cranberry grower. I understand he was a friend of yours. I want to ensure the correct person is charged for the crime, as I'm sure you do."

"I'm not talking about that. You need to leave."

"Tea." Larry startled Jake by speaking. Then he saw the big man's eyes wandering over to the gas cooktop. And the wisdom in what he said.

The woman stood perfectly still for a few beats, then her reluctance melted. "OK." She walked around Jake and Larry over to the cooktop, picked up a kettle, poured water from a Thermos, and set it on the flame. She pulled out three cups from the bottom shelf of one of the tables.

Jake shifted tactics. Rather than the direct approach, he decided to be more subtle. Sipping his tea, leaning against a fir tree, he started talking about himself, how he came to Long Beach to be the editor of the *Beachcomber*, about living in his RV, about meeting the sheriff, the niece of the murdered man.

He didn't expect her to respond, and she didn't. But she wasn't chasing them away, either.

"You keep a very well-policed camp," he offered, trying to establish some rapport, "better than I do in the motorhome. I got to wonder, though, what brought you to live here? These woods look like a scary place."

"I killed six men. Or seven."

Jake shifted his eyes towards Larry, who was as stoic as ever. Maybe coming deep into the woods with two people trained to kill wasn't the best idea.

Still, he was here. Might as well try to get the story. People generally wanted to talk, and a reporter was an excuse.

"Six or seven men?"

"Not like you might think," said Lanie, tossing the dregs of her cup beyond the perimeter of her camp.

And without looking at either Jake or Larry, she started to talk.

Lanie had been in the Army but not in combat. She was a highly trained radiation specialist. She worked at a base hospital in Germany, treating soldiers — often officers because they were older and more likely to contract one form of cancer or another. Her job was to operate the machine that zapped cancer cells.

Patients would come to her with a treatment plan, and she would set up the machine so the radiation hit the exact spot of cancer but nowhere else. Too much radiation, or too much in the wrong area, would kill healthy cells — and could kill the patient.

"We got a new doctor, Dr. Redbone, who specialized in treating colon cancer. He came from academia and was very smart and willing to let you know it. His idea was, along with zapping cancer in the colon, to expand the treatment area down the patients' bodies to the knees. He reasoned that since lymph nodes drain into the lower body, cancer cells could spread downward from the colon.

"I didn't think this was right, but I was a lowly tech, and

he was an officer and a doctor. So, I treated the patients the way he said.

"Many months after this new treatment started, I was having a beer with a friend who had transferred to Germany from the States. He told me about one of his patients who had developed infections from being over-radiated and died. And when he said the patient's name, I dropped my beer. It was my patient.

"I dug into the medical records of all the patients I treated for Dr. Redbone and discovered six had died because of infections caused by over-radiation.

"I went to him right away with the medical files. 'Close the door,' he told me when I got to his office. In a calm voice, he blistered my face with every profanity known to man — and Army officers know a lot of them — and ordered me to keep quiet. When I said I couldn't, he pulled a gun from his desk and shot me in the stomach."

She paused. A lone eagle issued a series of high-pitched whistles in the distance. The two men stood still, letting Lanie have a moment.

"When I woke in the hospital, I was told Dr. Redbone said I had tried to commit suicide and that he had saved me. But investigators already doubted his story, and when I reported what happened, he was taken into custody to face court-martial.

"Somehow, my story of how Dr. Redbone had me mistreat patients got into the press. The widow of one of the patients shot and killed Dr. Redbone as he was being walked into the court-martial.

"So, that's seven on my conscience.

"No more. No more. I can't do any harm out here. Whatever terrors these woods might hold are nothing to those in my mind."

CHAPTER 26

Jake sat on the edge of the small bed, Larry leaned against a tree, and Lanie occupied the lone chair as all three drank a second cup of tea in silence.

A poor reporter will badger a reluctant source. A so-so reporter will write a story saying the source wouldn't talk. A good reporter — and Jake was a good reporter — has a sense when a source wants to talk and waits for the words to come.

Once rapport had been established, as it had with Lanie, Jake knew half of her brain was arguing with the other half. Nothing he could say that she wouldn't tell herself more effectively.

The question for Jake was how to bring the argument to the correct conclusion.

"Well," he said, standing, "it's starting to get late, and I don't wish to be tripping over tree roots in the dark. It's probably time to head back. Is there anything I can tell the sheriff so the right man gets charged in the murder of your friend?"

"Blue hoodie. The person who killed Darrell was wearing a blue hoodie."

Lanie rested her head on cupped hands, elbows braced on her legs as she sat. "I had come down to talk. When the nightmares got too bad, I found that talking with Darrell would calm them down. He listened. He had buddies who had returned from Nam and knew the power of quiet listening. No suggestions, no advice, just listening.

"I had come around the bog on the way to his barn. He loved his man cave, all the old farming gewgaws, photos of cranberry harvesting in the early days, and signs with funny quotes about beer and stuff.

"I was just on the other side of the bog, where it narrows down, when I saw Darrell walk furiously out of the barn. Behind him, running, was a person in a blue hoodie, carrying a shovel or something. The person swung the shovel and caught Darrell just at the base of the neck. He went down immediately. The person in the hoodie dropped the shovel and raced off.

"I ran to Darrell but didn't need my medical training to see he was dead. The whole thing in Germany flashed through my head, and I ran off, too. Back to the forest, away from people who kill."

Jake wasn't so sure the forest was clear of people who kill.

"Lanie, this is vital information. Do you mind if I make a few notes?" She nodded, and he slipped out his reporter's notebook.

"Could you see their face?"

"Not in the rain. The person was short, shorter than Darrell, and he wasn't tall. I would say the person was also younger because they were agile in the swing and running away."

"Did Darrell say anything when you got to him?" Jake hated asking that question, but unasked questions have a way of biting back.

Lanie looked at Jake, held his gaze for a second, then shook her head.

Larry put his cup on the table, loud enough to signal it was time to go.

Goodbyes were said, and the men returned through the fir limbs to the trail, leaving Lanie in her private hell.

It wasn't until they broke into the clearing where his pickup was parked that Jake realized the one question he had failed to ask: Was the attacker a man ... or a woman?

CHAPTER 27

"Jake, you have to tell me who your source is. This is a murder investigation, not some TV show."

"I'm sorry, sheriff, but everything the source told me is in my story this week. The source doesn't want to go public."

Sheriff Ramblewood was shorter than Jake, but she presented an imposing figure when she puffed up, put her hands on her gun belt, and narrowed her eyes. Jake could see how average citizens could turn to jelly when faced with her authority.

She had burst into the office the first thing Thursday morning, holding the new edition of the *Beachcomber* with Lanie's story — although Lanie was only identified as "an unnamed source" in Jake's account.

But Jake was not an average citizen. He had been glared at before by larger figures than the sheriff.

In Jake's favor, Washington's shield law protected reporters who chose not to name their sources. But it had some exceptions. Was a capital offense an exception? Jake couldn't remember.

"Sheriff, the source will not talk to police and would not have talked to me if I were to reveal the name. You have more information than you had before. Go with that."

"I don't make threats. I make promises. If you don't tell me the source's name and how to contact this source, I will look into whether I can put you in jail until you reveal the name." After putting Jake on notice to get Lanie to come forward, the sheriff turned and left the *Beachcomber's* office.

"Wow, boss, if you go to jail, does that mean I get to run

the paper? I have some great ideas to make the paper more lively, less dull."

"I think this week is pretty lively, Bing, with John's story about people claiming a house based on Moroccan Law and my story saying a person in a blue hoodie killed the cranberry grower."

"Yeah, that's one week. Still, Bing's Bitches will probably be the best read in the paper. Did you see the one where one woman called out another for fooling around with her husband? Pure gold! Although it would have been better if you hadn't taken the names out."

"Call me stodgy, but with all that is going on right now, let's see if we can avoid a libel suit for a while."

*****

Jake had spent a few nights in jail years before, but the beer was involved along with young male stupidity. When his mother bailed him out, she didn't say a word. She just looked at him and shook her head sadly.

As he knew the sacrifices she had made to raise him as a single mom, he never got in that kind of trouble again.

Some reporters consider it a badge of honor to be jailed for protecting a source. Jake wasn't one of those. Most of the time, when he did the cops and courts beat for the Seattle *Times*, he got along fine with the police. He realized they had a tough — almost impossible — job in maintaining order in a society where disorder often gets a person his 15 minutes of fame on YouTube.

And, he liked Sheriff Ramblewood. She was a decent person trying to do her best for the community she grew up in. It was reasonable she would be incredibly diligent in trying to find the murderer of her uncle, the cranberry grower.

Yet, if he were in jail, the threatening man on the phone hunting Jessie might leave him alone.

But then... Bing would be running the paper. That wouldn't be good. Definitely not good. Maybe he should try to get

Lanie to go on the record.

"I'm back, Jake." Pat dropped her heavy purse on her desk, still holding a traveling coffee cup in her other hand. "Great front page this week."

"Welcome home. Did everything go OK with your daughter?"

"Yeah, all in all. I have good news and, well, other news."

She is probably going to quit, thought Jake. Maybe move to Yakima, where the girl's father lives. Better for the family, she'll say. That'll create an opening for a fresh reporter, maybe one of those kids from a smaller school, like Central or Eastern, who will work for peanuts and the experience. Some eager beaver who would generate piles of copy, maybe rough copy, but Jake could clean it up.

"On the way home — it takes like a freaking half of a day to get from Yakima to here — we had a long talk. I reflected on how much fun we used to have together — the mom-and-daughter family Carnation team — and how I missed that.

"She said that was part of the reason she left. She missed those days, too. She felt I had abandoned her lately by spending too much time on this job."

Here it comes, thought Jake. Look sad, tell her how much the paper will miss her, but don't beg her to stay. Turnover was always a struggle at a small paper, but new reporters bring fresh perspectives.

"I told her how much I loved my job, how much I loved meeting new people who were always doing the oddest things, and how no two days were alike. And it's true — I love coming to work at this newspaper.

"And then, together, we hit upon a brilliant idea. Although it might take you a moment to arrive at the same conclusion."

Jake reflexively folded his arms across his chest. "Brilliant idea? I always like brilliant ideas."

"My daughter is a junior, she'll be a senior next year. And you remember how little you learn as a senior in high school. No one is paying attention, their brains are already checked out.

"So, we are going to job share. I'll work 25 hours a week, and she'll work 15. Maybe more during the summer. That gives me time to be a mom around the home, and she'll get work experience, but more importantly, an insight into humanity.

"I can mentor her, help with the questions to ask, how to take notes, how newspapers organize stories, how to take photos."

Pat's excitement at the idea sparked from her hands as she waved the coffee cup around not so far from Jake.

"Some of the stories I do are so basic — the woman who had the collection of 1,000 sets of salt and pepper shakers, or the guy who grew the enormous watermelon for the county fair — they would be easy for her. And other stories, like interviews with the Junior Miss candidates, I'm so old to them and jaded. She could get lots of better information and quotes.

"So, what do you think?"

Aw, what the hell, thought Jake. First Bing's Bitches, now a high school reporter. What's it to me? The sheriff will probably have me locked away anyway.

"Sure, let's try it. Does she need a junior reporter press pass?"

CHAPTER 28

"Did you drop by with the name of your source?"

"No," said Jake, settling into the chair next to the sheriff's desk, "that situation hasn't changed. Can we let that sit for a moment and discuss a different case?"

"What different case? The Moroccan Law people? I told you that we are trying to contact the deeded owner of the property. We can't go in there without a complaint from them. County records show a corporation owns the property, but we don't have contact information. For all we know, the Moors are the real owners, and they just put up that sign as a prank."

"Yeah, I doubt that, but no. The case, or maybe not even a case, but a situation I'm interested in, is the deaths of the paper's previous owners, the McKinneys. Bing told me a little about how they died and said her sister, Mary Grace, a deputy with your department, thought there was something odd about it."

"Mary Grace." The sheriff paused. "She was a hire of the previous sheriff. She comes with a lot of opinions."

The sheriff pulled a folder from the bottom of a plastic tray on her desk. "But in this case, she may have a point."

"Bing said Miles was the driver and could have been intoxicated."

The sheriff flipped through papers in the folder. "Alcohol did appear in his blood work, but under the legal limit. Maybe one cocktail or glass of wine."

"She also said they were returning from a date night in Astoria."

"That's what we were told, too. It was Wednesday night,

and the week's edition was done. That's what you newspaper people do, right? Get one week's of work done, and then go out and celebrate."

Jake was about to defend having drinks when the paper came out, but considering how the sheriff said it, he thought it best to move on.

"I've driven that stretch of road to Astoria, and it's fairly straight on both sides of the short tunnel where the accident was. What do you suppose happened?"

"That is puzzling. It looks like they had just emerged from the tunnel, and then for some reason, Miles veered hard right, narrowly avoiding a guardrail and crashing into a tree. They likely were going pretty close to the speed limit on that stretch, but by not braking, they hit the tree at a fatal speed."

"And then the next day, a wrecked motorcycle was discovered?"

"Yes," said the sheriff, refreshing her memory by reading the file. "There's a little creek and a small pond the guardrail protects. Some kids were goofing around the next day, tossing rocks into the pond, when they saw a motorcycle. When we pulled it up, we also found the driver."

"Maybe the motorcycle had come into Miles' lane, and he reflexively veered to avoid him?"

"We thought that at first, too. But when accident investigators took a closer look at the car, they found the front end crushed by the tree, obviously, but the windshield was shoved in. And the polyvinyl — that thin layer of plastic between layers of the windshield that prevents it from shattering — displayed a rut, as if something had driven over it.

"Then we went back to look closer at the motorcycle. It was one of those fat tire motorcycles you see doing tricks at circuses and monster truck shows. We found bits of glass in the front tire.

"Now, I'm going to tell you a bit you can't report. Can you handle that, Mr. I can't reveal my sources?"

Jake was relieved the sheriff showed a sense of humor.

He may stay out of jail yet.

"OK. If you tell me something I need to print, I will ask you to repeat it on the record."

"This is where it gets baffling and, honestly, a little hard to believe, like something out of James Bond.

"To give her credit, deputy Mary Grace suggested it. She had seen riders on these trick motorcycles at shows rear them on the back wheel and drive over the top of oncoming cars. Like the stupidest, dumbest thing I can think of. Anyway, Mary Grace suggested the rider — on purpose — reared up on his back tire and drove over the hood of the McKinneys' car.

"Maybe, said Mary Grace, the motorcyclist was trying to cause the McKinneys to crash. Maybe this wasn't an accident but a murder. A double murder."

"Wow! Let me catch up," said Jake, furiously jotting in his reporter's notebook. "But then the motorcyclist ended up dead?"

"Yes. It had been raining hard that day. All that week. Again, Mary Grace. She theorized that in a usual trick like this, done in the dry confines of a stadium or dome, the motorcycle would travel straight over the car, down the back, and onto the road. But between the wet, slick roof of the car and the sudden jerk Miles made when he saw the motorcycle come over the hood, the tires slipped, and the driver lost control and was thrown into the pond. He drowned under the weight of the bike."

"And then we went back and looked at Miles' body. Now, this is the part you really can't even whisper about. You can print the rest of it, what I told you up to this point, but do not print this.

"Miles was mangled in the accident, and that's how we thought he died. But when the medical examiner looked closer, he found a small bullet wound, probably a .22 — downward into his chest. Miles was likely shot before the car hit the tree."

*****

On his way back from the sheriff's office, Jake ran through the interview he had just had and smiled. He was still a free man.

However, Sheriff Ramblewood's parting words to him were: "I've asked the prosecutor on a ruling whether I can arrest you for obstructing an investigation and jail you until you tell me the name of the person who witnessed my uncle's murder. I expect you not to leave town in the meantime."

Before that, the sheriff had also shared a couple of facts, neither of which she wanted to see in print. The first was a thorough search of the pond turned up a .22 pistol. The second was that while the driver didn't appear in FBI records of criminals, they got a match from Interpol. He was a former special forces soldier in the Russian army, a trick motorcycle rider, and had a police record as a mob enforcer.

"Why would a Russian mob enforcer want to kill a weekly newspaper publisher in Long Beach?"

The sheriff sighed. "Two words: Cranberry rustling."

When Jake asked for a further explanation, the sheriff said she had to go.

"Ask your reporter, John Ryan," she said, pulling her sidearm from a safe behind her desk and slipping it into her holster. "He's deep into the bizarre."

But Jake had another theory that had nothing to do with cranberry rustling.

CHAPTER 29

It was Saturday morning, and Jake had nothing to do but lie in bed, admiring the sleeping beauty of Ruby.

Her red hair curled across the pillow she had puffed up under her head, wine-red fingernails wrapped into a fist under her chin, and pleasant sleeping noises bubbled from her mouth. He would never tell a woman she snored, but in his experience, women make little noises telling you they are pleasantly deep in slumberland.

Sex was great with Ruby — sex was fabulous with Ruby — but sex can be a weak glue in a relationship.

For some reason, Jake thought of when he was a young teen and built a little boat out of balsa wood, holding the pieces together with white Elmer's glue he had for school projects. He purchased a tiny outboard motor powered by a small battery to place on the stern panel of the boat and took the whole thing down to a pond in a nearby park.

He was so proud of his little boat, designed after a Chris-Craft cabin cruiser he saw in *Life* magazine, and thought it would be so cool to watch it speed across the water, the little propeller on the replica outboard engine spinning hard, powering the boat along.

And it was cool when he carefully placed the boat in the water and switched on the engine with a fingernail.

Here was something he made himself, with no help from his mom or anyone else. He drew up the design, purchased and then cut up the balsa wood to exact specifications, found the engine at a hobby shop, which he paid for himself, and then assembled the pieces into a finished working model.

He was the only kid he knew who had done something like this. He proudly wrote a name on the side with a magic marker: USS Jake.

As Jake watched the boat speed across the pond, the stern board slowly came loose from the sides and was pushed into the cabin by the engine's thrust. The little propeller spun wildly, pointing uselessly straight up.

The little cabin cruiser collapsed into the water when the sides fell away. Dumbstruck, Jake saw the individual pieces floating on the water, too far from shore for him to retrieve.

It took a few days for the forlorn Jake to tell his mom about his disaster.

"Oh, honey, you used Elmer's glue? That's made for paper. If you put it in water, it turns into liquid and loses its adhesion. You could have painted it, that would have protected the glue."

Thinking about the boat misadventure now, while next to the sleeping Ruby, Jake made an analogy that if sex was the glue that first bonded their relationship, then all the moments in between coated the relationship with staying power.

The way she laughed at his jokes or easily dropped a vocabulary word into the conversation — he always had a thing for intelligent women — or brought a piece of pie home from the diner she thought he might like built the little moments into something precious and robust.

"Jake, are you staring at me?"

Ruby's question brought him to attention. "Enamored with your beauty, you mean? Yes, I was. Like engrossed in looking at the Mona Lisa."

"She was 25. I'm not." Softening her tone, she added, "She was also fully dressed. I'm not."

Jake got the hint, and thoughts of balsa wood boats went right out of his mind.

*****

"Let's have some fun today."

"I kinda thought that was fun."

"Yes, yes, it was. I mean, let's get out and do something. My shift at the restaurant starts late. You're not working now, right?"

Jake had considered going in to write next week's editorial while the office was quiet on Saturday morning, but the office would be silent on Sunday, too.

"Nope, nothing on my plate."

"You have those new hiking shoes. Maybe we should go on a nature walk in the woods."

Jake flashed on the tripping over roots, being hit in the face with low-hanging limbs, slipping on thick moss covering slippery mud, and the sound of a shotgun being racked during his hike with Larry to interview Lanie.

"Maybe the ground is still a little wet for a nature walk. How about we go out for a seafood lunch?"

"Ugh! I'm around food all day at the diner. We could take one of those whale-watching boat excursions."

Jake's ill-fated boat-building project leaped back into his brain, as did images of the disassembled craft floating on the water.

"When I breezed through the winter tourist section the paper does, I saw the best time for whale watching is December through mid-February. We've missed that."

"We're avoiding the obvious — let's go for a long walk along the beach. Isn't that what they always say in those singles ads — seeking a partner who enjoys long walks on the beach."

"Great idea," said Jake, "and I can still wear my new hiking boots."

*****

Watching the endless waves roll onto the nearly flat sandy beach, with the sun parked just behind thin layers of clouds, his girl at his side, Jake could understand the allure of a beach walk.

Maybe they should move to a tropical island, where the weather was always balmy and the ocean warm enough to swim in. Undoubtedly, the local paper would need a journalist like him, and Ruby appeared sufficiently adaptable to fit into various jobs.

He was about to suggest the idea when she snuggled up against his side and asked, "Have you found anything more about Big Red's fortune? What did you find in Jane's things?"

"I couldn't find anything in the archives about what happened to Big Red. Honestly, the archives are a mess. And then, when I asked Adele about what Jane left behind, Adele said they mainly consisted of ad call sheets and designs for spec ads.

"Except, there was one metal file box with a lock. Adele said she didn't find a key, plus figured it likely was something personal, not related to ads in the newspaper. Maybe something to do with the newspaper's sale. Anyway, she gave me the file box, but I haven't had a chance to try to open it."

"I bet I could open it. I'm pretty good at that sort of stuff. Let's go try." She pulled her arm free of Jake and turned around.

"It's so pretty out here. This is my first time walking the famous beach since we came to town. Don't you want to walk some more?"

"Sand, waves, squawking gulls. I've seen enough for today. Come on, let's look at that box. Maybe there are clues inside. Clues to a mystery, doesn't that excite you, Mr. Newspaperman?"

*****

Jake pulled the metal box from his desk's footwell and placed it on his desk. Now he took a good look, he saw it was made out of sturdier metal than the typical file box. And the lock looked more serious, too.

Ruby pulled a bobby pin from her flowing hair and, just like the movies, started twisting it in the lock, a rosebud tip of her tongue protruding from one side of her mouth.

"There!"

She placed her hands on both sides of the lid and lifted it.

Dozens of tabbed file folders appeared, leaning front to back. "The notations on the tabs, they're not in English," said Jake.

"That's Russian, I believe."

"You read Russian?"

"I have had to learn bits and pieces of several languages."

She straightened the files to the front, revealing the bottom rear of the box.

"Jake!"

"Stop!" She had been reaching for a black revolver. "We should think about our next steps. Maybe we should turn this over to the sheriff."

"Yes, we could do that. But we have no reason to think that gun is involved in a crime or anything. Maybe we should take a look at some of these files first."

Before Jake could say anything, she reached into the first folder and pulled out a folded map, which she quickly spread on Jake's desktop. A few fragments from the old map came loose and fell on the floor.

"Look, there's the beach. These little squares appear to be houses overlooking the beach. Only there are not near as many houses that are there today. And some of the houses have red parallel lines between them. Could this have something to do with Big Red?"

"When telling the smuggler's story, John Ryan said he moved between houses secretively. Maybe he used tunnels."

A flash lit up the map.

"What are you doing? Why did you take a photo of the map?"

Sliding her iPhone into her back pocket, Ruby shrugged. "Just in case something should happen to the map, we will have a copy. No worries. Now, let's look at some of the other folders."

But the flash from the camera had set off a warning in Jake. If Ruby could read Russian, and he couldn't, she might not tell Jake everything she had learned. He'd have to figure out how to read the files first.

"Let's wait. Your shift at the diner begins in a few minutes. And I need to work on next week's editorial. Let's let Big Red's secret stay a secret for a little while longer."

CHAPTER 30

"Sheriff, you can use all the euphemisms you want, but there is no way to avoid saying one of your deputies tasered a man in his balls."

"She did it to protect one of your employees, Jake."

"Yes, I'm grateful Bing wasn't injured. From what I heard, Bing was handling herself perfectly fine until her sister, Deputy Mary Grace, came along and deliberately shot a taser dart into the testicle area of the guy shouting at her."

"Jake, I will defend my officers to the hilt. Deputy Mary Grace is an experienced member of this police department. She is well-trained in the use of force. If she tasered someone, my first reaction is that someone had it coming. The shot to the balls," Sheriff Ramblewood quickly suppressed a smile that flew across her face, "resulted from a quickly evolving and unstable situation. Maybe her aim was off."

"Hey, you two, can I suggest we adhere to the language in the press release I wrote," said undersheriff Snyder, who intervened to cool down his boss and Jake. "Lower central quadrant is a more family-friendly, precise term."

Both the sheriff and Jake turned to glare at Snyder, who kept any further suggestions to himself.

"Jake, we will review this incident as we review all incidents of shooting, taser, or otherwise. Appropriate action will be taken, should that be the findings. In the meantime, I strongly urge the paper not to make a big issue about this. Let the process work."

"Let the process work? A guy in a t-shirt, shorts, and flip-flops was tasered by a deputy on the main street, right in front of Ruby's Diner on the first sunny tourist-friendly Saturday afternoon we have had in about forever here. Not only has the newspaper received half a dozen photos of him rolling around on the sidewalk, holding his 'central lower quadrant' area, but it's also trending on social media under the hashtag 'Please deputy, don't taser my balls.'

"I think we are beyond not making a big issue of this."

"OK, OK." The sheriff sighed. "How about this: We have been holding back key information on the mill fire. We have some evidence out to the state crime lab. I am expecting to hear the results tomorrow. How about I share that information with the *Beachcomber* tomorrow in time to make your Wednesday print deadline? If you deem that news important enough, maybe you could not find space on your front page for pictures of the tasering?"

Jake was no virgin to trading favors with the police. In his experience, most good officers wanted the public to know and understand the gray areas that went along with keeping order. Only the bad officers preferred operating in the dark, or the political wannabes spun every sentence out of their mouths.

"We've been beaten by social media so badly on this story, I would be happy to keep it off the front page. I could even ignore it were it not for one of our employee's involvement."

"Speaking of that, this was Bing's fault. Her Bitches column is stirring the pot. You should speak to her about responsible journalism."

A smile started in the sheriff's eyes. "You know, Jake, if you don't give me the name of the witness to Darrell's murder, and if Bing keeps causing public disturbances, you two may end up sharing a cell here."

*****

"Oh, boss, this is so good for the paper!"

Bing was giddy with emotion when Jake returned from his Monday morning with Sheriff Ramblewood. So excited, Jake noticed that she called him boss for the first time.

"Bing, we need to talk...."

Bing had no time to listen. "Everybody, and I mean everybody, will read next week's Bing's Bitches. That column is dynamite! People care about what's in the paper again! You know what? We could sell ads around my column. And charge a premium!"

Bing hurried over to Adele, who was mapping out her ad call list for the week, to share her idea.

"I heard the call on the police scanner," said Pat from her desk. "From the description of the encounter, the man was explosive."

"I've heard bits and pieces. Were you there?"

"Yes," said Pat, as usual, staring over Jake's shoulder. "The man was furious at Bing and confronted her on the street. She had an item in her column that he was cheating on his girlfriend. The girlfriend — when she read the item — kicked him out. Then, to make matters worse, the woman he cheated with also kicked him out once she discovered he had been living with his girlfriend. She thought they were exclusive."

"I edited that column. I don't recall any names. How did all the players know who was being referred to?"

"Baby Whale. The man's nickname is Baby Whale, and that nickname was in the column. He has a smiling baby whale tattooed on his... member."

"Ewww, ouch! I don't want to imagine that. Or the pain of getting that done. So, was Bing in any danger from the man?"

"Bing in danger? I think she was about to kick the man in his baby whale when her sister, the deputy, showed up. Mary Grace has a rumored history of excessive force, except no guy wants to report getting roughed up by a woman, so she gets away with it. She probably aimed for the baby whale and hit his pods instead."

CHAPTER 31

This week's paper looked strong on Monday afternoon as Jake penciled in stories.

There would be an update on page one revealing the startling Russian mobster connection to the McKinneys' deaths, a sweet but sad interview with their two surviving sons by Pat, and whatever the sheriff had on Tuesday morning about the mill fire.

John Ryan was actually at his desk, pounding out an update on the Moroccan Law squatters — the second group of Moors was claiming a house adjacent to the first group — and a reader had submitted a photo of the sun reflected in a water puddle, foretelling good weather had arrived.

Other readers had submitted photos of Mr. Baby Whale writhing in the street after being tasered in the privates. Once Jake got past his empathic discomfort, he had to admit the shots were funny. He penciled in the best image for the expanded two pages he dedicated to Bing's Bitches, which he slotted for the rear of the paper. Even back there, the pages would still likely be the best read of the edition.

Drop in a couple of pages for high school sports — the girls were still winless in softball, but the boys were headed to the district baseball playoffs — and the paper was complete.

"I have great news, Mr. Stewart!"

Brandi had just turned old enough to drink legally, but she still looked like a kid when she bounced to Jake's desk. And, to her, he must have looked like a relic because she had never gotten past calling him Mr. Stewart.

"What is it?" he asked the paper's part-time ad designer.

"I got a graphics job in Seattle! And it's my dream job, doing exactly what I want to do with a growing software game company. I'll have a great boss, work with people my age on the cutting edge of technology, and get stock options. And I'll be living in Seattle, not my mother's house!"

"Well, good for you! Hmmm… we'll have to find another ad designer. When do you leave?"

"My boss wants me there right away. Like today."

"OK, so soon. You'll give us a couple of weeks to interview and hire someone?"

"No. Like today. I'm going home to pack and leaving this afternoon for Seattle. Can I have my final check now?"

"Brandi, you can't leave without giving us time to find a replacement, and that will be difficult in even two weeks. I don't know what the labor market is like here. How about we get through this week — I'll place a help-wanted ad in this week's edition — and you take off next Tuesday after all the ads are done?"

Brandi shook her head. "This is my dream job. I'm leaving now, but I need my check. Can I have it, please?"

"Brandi, I know you're young, and this new job sounds thrilling, but you can't leave an employer in the lurch. Your new boss will understand you taking an extra week. He must have people leaving too and will appreciate your ethics in giving fair notice."

Brandi's face darkened. "He said he needs me tomorrow. I need gas money. Why are you being so stubborn? The gaming world moves at cutting edge speed, not like…" she paused to look around at the mismatched surplus store desks, piles of papers in the corners, the disheveled John Ryan banging out a story using only two fingers, "an old weekly newspaper."

"Let her go. We don't have that many ads this week anyway." Adele, the ad salesperson, had come over to Jake's desk.

"Sure, OK." He turned towards Bing, who was already writing a check from the business ledger, "Bing, make it for half a day today."

Jake was immediately sorry for his smallness, but why should the paper be generous? From his experience running newspapers, Jake was slowly changing his attitude from thinking the bosses were always wrong to now thinking employees could be selfish and a pain.

Brandi took the check from Bing, grabbed her jacket from the office coat rack, and left.

A hush settled over the office, the only sound the rattling of John's keyboard being abused by two fingers.

*****

"Jake, I just talked to my daughter. She wants to do Brandi's job."

"Your 14-year-old daughter? I thought she wanted to be a reporter with her mom, team Carnation?"

"She's 16. I sent her out on one story, and she bombed. She is so mouthy at home but became tongue-tied when interviewing a woman about her prize Chinese Foo Dog. She got the basic facts wrong — she wrote the dogs were bred to guard movie stars rather than temples — and that the owner 'b-a-l-l-e-d with pleasure' when her dog won first place in a dog show, rather than 'b-a-w-l-e-d,'" said Pat in spelling out the similar words that had totally different meanings.

"We agreed maybe reporting was not her thing. But she is excited to work at the newspaper, like her mom. And all high school kids are taught basic graphic programs on the computer, so she thinks she could handle designing ads here. Besides, she wants to save up to buy a car. Can you give her a try?"

"Let's bring her in." Jake thought of a pun involving "balling with pleasure at the new job" and "bawling" but didn't think a mother of a 16-year-old girl would want to hear it.

CHAPTER 32

"OK, Jake, I have breaking news for you on the mill fire, but we are clear on the tasering photo, correct?"

Sheriff Ramblewood sat in the chair beside Jake and leaned in, an arm over a file she had placed on the editor's desk. As promised, she had come in early Tuesday morning.

"Yes, the paper is running a photo, but it doesn't show deputy Mary Grace, and it's in the back of the paper." He didn't mention it was with this week's Bing's Bitches column, likely the most popular pages in the paper. No point in getting the sheriff sidetracked.

"I have a press release and photos we'll release Wednesday afternoon. I'm willing to share them early because of your deadline — I want you to know I value the department's relationship with the hometown newspaper."

Jake knew that a week ago, the daily newspaper in Longview, about 70 miles away, had run an editorial pointing out the sudden jump in crime in Pacific County and wondered if the female sheriff and her small department were up to the task of maintaining public order.

Jake also knew the *Beachcomber* had a better circulation in Pacific County than the Longview daily — as he was sure the sheriff knew that fact, too — and since her office was elected, keeping on the right side of local media was good politics.

"One more thing. You remember what I want to be kept off the record about Miles' and Jane's deaths?"

"Yes." She was referring to the gunshot wound inflicted by a Russian mob enforcer. The story the paper had this week of a motorcycle purposefully crashing into the former publishers, leading to their deaths, was explosive enough. He could easily hold the gunshot detail back. It would justify another front-page story — a series of explosive stories was better than just a single story.

"OK, so after the fire at the mill, we brought in state arson investigators. I'm casting no aspersions on the mill owners — this is standard practice in fires of businesses where significant insurance policies are involved.

"The inspectors didn't find conclusive evidence of arson, but they think the fire started in the office area, where they found a body deep in the ashes. We did a quick search for local missing persons, especially anyone with a connection to the mill. No mill employee and no one from the family that owns the mill was missing.

"Who was it who died from the fire? How did he die? What was he doing at the mill?"

"He died from a bullet in the brain. We have no idea why he was at the mill. And neither do the owners. And at first, we didn't know who he was."

"Wow!" Jake quickly typed the sheriff's words into his computer.

"Since he wasn't a local missing person, I kept the information quiet to see who or what happened next. The information from the state crime lab returned this morning — DNA results confirm he was a Russian man with international gang links."

"Sheriff…"

"Yes, I know there could be a link to Miles' and Jane's murders. But I don't want that out there yet, OK?

"I know I'm asking a lot. And while I have threatened Deputy Mary Grace with firing if she says a word about the investigation, I have known her since high school. She will not be able to keep a lid on her mouth, especially since she was the one who developed the crime theory on the McKinneys' deaths, which is proving to be true."

"I'll honor our deal," Jake stopped typing, "but the news

is a competitive commodity. It's only good when it's fresh. I don't want to be beaten."

"The newspaper's needs and wants are not my problems. My priority is keeping local citizens safe and Russian mobsters out of my county. I'll keep the media informed the best I can but not at the jeopardy of not doing my job the way I think it should be done."

*****

After the sheriff left, John Ryan drifted over to Jake's desk, rapidly typing the story about the body in the mill.

"I guess it's going to be up to the paper to break this case wide open."

"You heard about the Russian's body in the mill?" asked Jake.

"All of it. There is a bigger story for next week. We'll talk later. I'll meet you tonight at the usual place."

CHAPTER 33

"My first wife was Russian, well, not my first wife. My first wife was a practice wife, so the Russian was, I guess, my second wife. But she was a dandy."

John Ryan stopped talking, and Jake knew what that meant. He laid a $5 bill on the bar and glanced up to see Velma already pouring golden liquid into a short glass over ice.

Jake and John met at the Green Hornet to talk about their next move in the puzzling case of the Russian mobsters.

John Ryan took a sip. "She was also a beauty. She was a woman who looked better than she photographed, and she photographed very nicely because all I saw of her was a photo before I proposed, and then when she showed up, she made the picture look like trash. She dazzled.

"I was surprised she would be attracted to a man like me, although I was pretty handsome and a bit of a he-man in those days.

"I was also surprised to see a four-year-old boy with her. She hadn't mentioned the boy in the ad. Maybe she had counted on her looks to slip the boy by. I didn't care. I liked children back then.

"This was before all of the online stuff people do now. We had an arranged marriage, arranged by a broker who matched Russian women to men in the West.

"I wrote to her I was going homesteading in Alaska and wanted a mate to keep me warm in the wilds. I'm ashamed to say those words now, but I was full of myself in those days," said John, nursing his drink.

Velma slid an Irish Death across the bar to Jake. He was

trying something new, and the dark-named brew from central Washington felt right.

"She wrote that she would be eager and excited to go to Alaska. I think any young woman in Russia in those days would have been eager and excited to be somewhere else.

"So, after a fall and winter in Seattle, off we went in the early spring, the three of us. Soon to be four. I said she was beautiful, but she also possessed a vibrant personality. Bright and talented, too. She had performed classical music in concert halls on grand pianos across Russia.

"I had chosen a spot just north of the Arctic Circle to homestead, where a man can be a man.' Young men can be so stupid." John grimaced and slowly shook his head. He shifted his empty glass back and forth in his knobby fingers.

Another $5 was laid down, and another full glass slid his way.

"The one thing she insisted on for going to Alaska was to bring a piano. Not a grand piano as in concert halls, but a baby grand piano. It's still a damn big thing, I can tell you.

"I had found a cabin on a piece of land that had been abandoned by a previous back-to-the-lander just north of Fort Yukon, and we settled in there, me, her, the boy, and the person growing inside her.

"By late summer, we had harvested our crop of vegetables, I had laid in cords of wood, and the baby had arrived. All was looking good as winter approached.

"And what a winter it was. Some 20, 30, and 40 degrees below zero, days on end. But we got through that. To occupy myself, I built a wooden cradle for the baby. I was pretty handy with wood tools then.

"Spring was approaching, and boy, were we relieved! Then bang! Another cold front moved in and stayed on. We had electricity where we were, but winds blew trees over the power lines, leaving us in the dark and cold.

"All we had for heat was a wood stove. Soon, the wood I had laid in the past fall was gone, and the temperatures were still cold, oh, bone-chilling cold. All the furniture in the house was made of wood, so I took a hatchet and started hacking apart kitchen chairs, the table, a sofa, and then our marriage bed. I hesitated for as long as possible, but my family was freezing, so the beautiful cradle was fed into the stove.

"I was like a madman, wandering room to room, hatchet in hand, looking for wood to feed into the fire. My family huddled under blankets as close as possible to the stove — now starved for wood."

By now, the tavern had gone silent, and ears turned towards John. Even Velma stood motionless on her side of the bar, hanging onto every word.

"All that remained in the living room was the piano. The 500-pound baby grand piano.

"I looked at my family, my beautiful wife, the five-year-old boy I had grown to love, and the baby still in his mother's arms. All in danger of freezing to death. And I looked at that piano, so much wood it could burn for days.

"I brought the hatchet up to strike the first blow. '*Nyet!*' she yelled. I looked into her eyes, and I saw... I saw that striking that piano would end us as a family. They say women can be tough. Russian women are the toughest of them all.

"But I wasn't that tough. I wasn't willing to risk my family for art. I brought the hatchet down, and soon that piano was nothing but firewood.

"We survived, of course. That piano fed the fire for the next couple of days, and then the power came back on. But come spring, she was gone.

"All I have left is a story... and the ability to speak a little Russian."

CHAPTER 34

On Wednesday mornings, Jake liked to linger around the RV, have a second cup of coffee, and take a leisurely shower.

Bing was still at the press, so she wouldn't be in the office to not so subtly look at her wristwatch when he came in past 9 a.m. Not only wasn't Bing his boss, but Jake hadn't collected a paycheck up to this point. He sometimes felt more like a volunteer at the paper than the boss.

Still, she seldom missed an opportunity to make him feel like a slacker.

"Hey, I'm turning on the water heater," he announced, hitting the toggle switch. Water was only heated in an RV when it was needed. Otherwise, it would burn through all the propane quickly. "It'll take 20 minutes. Any ideas on what to do in the meantime?"

A giggle indicated Ruby did indeed have an idea.

*****

A leisurely shower in an RV is different than a leisurely shower in a house. The hot water tank in the Hulk held only three gallons, which meant Jake would spray water over his head, face, and pits, then turn off the water to shampoo up.

He would then rinse by spraying around the shower nozzle on its flexible hose, turn off the water again, and soap up the rest of his body.

The leisurely part came in this second rinsing, eyes closed, moving the massaging spray around his body, easing minor pains and tensions, until a few minutes later, the water turned cool.

When he turned off the water, he heard a visitor's voice from the front of the RV.

"Missy, do you have Bailey's to go with this coffee? I sometimes like a kick in the morning."

"No Bailey's but Kahlua. It's a coffee liqueur with a touch of rum."

"OK, I guess that will have to do. I'll take two sunny-side-up eggs and a few of those hash browns I see you making. No more than half a muffin... all right, a whole muffin, I wouldn't want to waste the second half.

"Hey, Mr. Editor Man," she said, raising her voice, "you taking a spa day in there? I thought today was a work day?"

"Hi, Mary Teresa," Jake said through the toilet/shower area door, adding, "Ruby, can you please hand me my clothes."

"Oh, Mr. Editor Man, don't worry about me. I've seen it before." Lowering her voice, she said to Ruby, "And it's not near the sight they think it is, is it, Missy?"

Cracking the door, Ruby shoved through clothes Jake had set on the bed, her face red from holding in laughter.

"While we're waiting for Mr. Clean and Shiny, how about sliding a few more hash browns my way, Missy? You've made them crisp, as they should be, not limp, like..." she raised her voice to make sure Jake heard, "...some men I know." She chuckled at her joke.

"Mary Teresa, what brings you around this morning?" Jake maneuvered in the tight RV hallway past Ruby, who was grating another potato to start over on the hash browns.

"Mr. Editor Man, you've been here long enough. You need to start doing your job and save this town."

CHAPTER 35

After Mary Teresa left, Ruby relit the burners to start a second breakfast, as the early morning visitor pretty well cleaned out the first one.

Grating another batch of spuds, she said, "Jake, I've been looking at Jane's map of Big Red's homes. Some of them have red X's through them."

"What?" Ruby's comment brought Jake quickly out of deep thoughts about Mary Teresa's challenge. "How did you get the map?"

"I took a photo of it. Remember?" She pushed the hash browns to one side of the skillet, making room for a couple of strips of bacon.

"I think the McKinneys, or maybe just Jane, thought these homes might be the hiding place for the silver treasure, but she somehow investigated them and found nothing. So, she crossed them off her list." She slid half a portion of hash browns onto each of the two plates, adding four eggs to the pan.

"You've been studying the map? You haven't said anything."

"Yeah, I guess I have caught the treasure finder bug. Haven't you thought about it?" She laughed, flipping the eggs. "Wouldn't it be a hoot if we found the treasure? And if it's all in silver coins, it would be untraceable. Do you want more coffee with breakfast?"

Jake held back from admitting he had been thinking about the bootlegger's fabled treasure. He was thinking about it a lot, in fact.

More than thinking about it, he had researched silver

coins on Google and found in the 1920s and '30s, the most popular silver coins were the Peace silver dollars, with Lady Liberty on the front and an American eagle on the flip side.

They were still accepted for general use, but the real value was selling to collectors, who would pay anywhere from $6 to $35, depending on quality.

Since any coins secreted away would be uncirculated, their quality would likely be excellent. Even a modest treasure from the 1930s would be worth 20 to 30 times that amount today.

Suddenly, the notion the McKinneys had purchased the *Beachcomber* as a cover for finding the treasure didn't seem so far-fetched. Miles could ask questions as a reporter and get into places off-limits to the average person. And Jane's flashy looks and personality would also open doors.

And what they may have been near finding could also have been a motive for their murders.

"And another thing I found," said Ruby, bringing Jake out of his reverie by pulling up the map on her phone, "is this spot with a circle. See where it is?" She held the phone out to Jake.

"It's too small for me to see."

"Yeah, we need to look at the original map again. But this spot," she used her fingers to expand the map on the phone, "is near where the old ferry docked before they built the bridge to Astoria."

"There was a ferry across the Columbia River to Astoria in Oregon?"

"Yes, it ran for decades before the bridge was built in 1962. Haven't you read the history special section the *Beachcomber* puts out? Customers at the diner leave it, and I look it over during my breaks. This area has a fascinating history and some fascinating characters. Lots of tough guys and wheeling and dealing."

Ruby made the map larger and smaller on the phone, trying to get a fix on the location of the red circle. "Didn't Bing say the McKinneys were returning from a date night in Astoria when they were killed? Maybe their date night wasn't going to dinner in Astoria but searching for this place. I wonder what they found and how we can find it?"

How "we" can find it? reflected Jake. In his dreaming about the treasure, there was no "we," just him. He was just limping along financially with good-paying jobs in the newspaper business drying up and his severance running low from his career at the Seattle Times. And so far, the *Beachcomber* wasn't kicking in anything to his kitty.

Changing careers to becoming a distributor of rare coins sounded like a cozy transition to whatever was to come next.

"Well, I got to run. I've become a boring girl from making breakfast for you to serving breakfast at the diner."

"Oh no, Ruby," Jake laughed, "you are not boring at all."

When she closed the RV door behind her, Jake was still smiling about how lucky he was that she had come serendipitously into his life.

But wait. Was it serendipitous? A woman meets a man at a gas station and hops into his RV a few seconds later? Maybe a desperate, runaway teenage girl might be so naive, but an adult woman who's been around in the world? Not likely.

And the way she got into bed with him? Sure, like any guy, he's prone to think of himself as a sex magnet. But he's also old enough to know the difference between reality and fantasy. And a beautiful, intelligent woman like Ruby climbing into his bed on the first night is the stuff of testosterone-fed dreams.

And now her staying with him in the RV, making no sounds about moving out, saying nothing about her past life, working as a waitress — could that be a cover job?

And how did she know the markings on Jane's file box folders were in Russian? He didn't recognize the strange script, and he's a journalist who knows a little about everything. She said she had been around and just learned a smattering of Russian. She was also eager to look inside the folders, but how would her "smattering" of Russian be able to read documents?

And now, the way she cleverly showed Jake a location to

investigate. Did she want him along as a fellow treasure hunter — or as protection in case the Russian mob guys returned?

How much could he trust Ruby? Isn't Ruby just another name for red, like in Big Red? Was he being played for a fool?

CHAPTER 36

"I have two tickets to an autopsy Saturday night, and unlike the revolution, it will be televised."

"What are you talking about, John?" Jake was at his desk Wednesday, penciling in the stories for next week's edition but more focused on working out the challenge Mary Teresa had laid down. And the puzzle of Ruby.

"The revolution will not be televised?" John moved to the center of the newsroom, between the desks, and, looking up, began reciting:

> The revolution will not be televised
> The revolution will not be brought to you
> By Xerox in four parts without commercial interruptions...

Pausing for breath, he ran a hand over his bald dome and reflected: "It's been 50 years since Mr. Gil Scott-Heron wrote that call to arms, but I can still feel the power. I was a street-fighting man in those days, manning the barricades, waving the signs, yes, I will admit it, throwing a few rocks. In the streets during the day," winking towards Pat, "and at night, between the sheets...."

"John, the autopsy. What are you talking about?"

"That's what I'm saying, it will be televised. And I have tickets for both of us."

"Why do I want to go to an autopsy, televised or not?"

"Because, my young friend who grew up in strangely non-political times, you are the one who first discovered the story. And then left it up to me, the veteran investigative reporter on the staff, to dig out the truth. Oh, 'dig out' and 'autopsy,' probably a pun there, but you better avoid it in headlines."

John retreated to his desk, grabbed a wrinkled all-weather jacket draped over his chair, and headed for the door. "Time to hit the streets again, see what trouble I can stir up."

"The only thing he's going to stir up is the dust on a bar stool," muttered Pat, just loud enough for Jake to hear.

*****

"Jake, can you talk?"

Newspaper broker Dave Raymond had called Jake at the *Beachcomber* office, and as usual, he wanted to be cautious about any of his words leaking out. Dave said he liked to keep news about a possible sale hush-hush — "it can scare away advertisers and send your best employees looking for other jobs," he had said.

Jake figured it was more a superstition, as in Jake's experience, the best way to sell anything was to announce it loudly and widely.

"Sure, Dave, we can talk. Do you have a buyer lined up?"

"In truth, it's going a little slow. I once had a newspaper listed in Alaska that took three years to sell. You have to be patient."

"Three years? That's beyond patience. What about the former owner? He has money from the sale. Maybe he misses the business."

"Old man Corcoran? I hear he traveled to Korea, looking for a wife, then got into a quarantine situation and is in lockdown there. Besides, I have never seen a seller so happy, he even kissed me when I delivered the check. I had never had a man kiss me before, not even when I was in the Air Force, stationed with all guys flying missions over China's mainland. The government denied flying over Red China in the 1950s, but let me tell you, we were up every day, bombs in the bay and sophisticated spy cameras on board. Since then, I've never believed the government when...."

"Dave, about a sale. I heard a Canadian chain is buying up coastal papers in the state. How about approaching them?"

"The Vancouver group? They are good operators and can turn a small cash flow into a flood. But they also rob a paper of its soul. I don't think the McKinneys would be happy with a sale to soulless Canadians."

"Dave, not to be too harsh, the McKinneys are dead. And their sons are too young to care what happens to the paper. Some money from the Canadians is better than nothing. Besides, we have several big stories breaking that could rattle the community. We need flesh and blood publishers who can make key decisions they can live with."

"Oh, no, Jake, I wouldn't rattle the community. Play it safe. Keep the paper alive, and make a profit. Don't upset the employees, and most of all, please the readers. I have to go to my Rotary meeting now. Remember, be like a clam, don't make waves."

And with that, Dave was gone.

"Don't make waves?" Jake was a newspaperman. He was born to make waves.

Despite Dave's parting comment and thinking of Mary Teresa's challenge this morning, Jake decided that the *Beachcomber* needed not safer reporting but more sensational reporting.

Even if that meant attending his first televised autopsy.

CHAPTER 37

"If I write a story that helps solve a crime, do I get the reward money?"

"What are you talking about, Pat?"

"My daughter is still in school, right? The kids have been talking about the track coach and the murder of the cranberry grower. They developed a theory that sounds pretty reasonable to me. I could run it down and maybe turn it into a story."

"Yeah, that's your job." Jake's annoyance crept through into his voice. What happened to reporters just reporting instead of looking for big payoffs?

"The cranberry growers have put up a $25,000 reward for information that results in an arrest in the murder. My story could lead to an arrest, not of the coach, but of someone else. Could I collect the reward? I could use the money to pay for my daughter's college. God knows, her dad won't be able to kick in any money."

"In truth, Pat, I've never encountered this question before. Thinking about it, if we get the story first, and then you make a separate arrangement with the cranberry growers, then good for you. But let's be clear: your job is to write stories readers want to read, not to write stories for potential reward money."

"Big papers pay for stories all the time. I'm just cutting out the middle man."

"As far as I know, we never paid for stories at the *Seattle Times*. I think only trashy papers like the supermarket gossip sheets pay for stories. You know, the queen's maid blabs about the queen's incontinence issues and dishes dirt on the royal kids."

But in truth, Jake also knew big papers dealt favors for stories. If a realtor passed along a tidbit about a Hollywood star buying an expensive lakefront home, that realtor wouldn't be named as the source but would get a mention about handling the sale, a sure way for the realtor to attract more business.

Jake wondered what was happening to his ethics: first Bing's Bitches, then agreeing to hold back details on local murders and now letting a reporter write a story for possible cash rewards.

Maybe there was a reason journalists were rated just above used car salespeople for their trustworthiness. Or was it just below?

*****

"You might see me as an old fat white guy on a Harley, but I'm much more than that. I'm also a thinker."

To Jake, the man crunching down the chair next to the editor's desk did look white, old, and fat, and since he was wearing black leathers and Jake had heard the distinctive roar of a Harley rumble up to the street outside the office, a motorcycle rider.

The "thinker" part was, as of yet, left uncertain.

"I got a book in me, and slowly, page by page, I am squeezing it out. I call myself, The Motorcycle Philosopher. I have a message to the people of the world, and I want you to publish it for me."

"Hmmm… we do more local books, like, *Biggest Trees of Pacific County*, see over there?" Jake pointed to a display of books the *Beachcomber* had printed over the years.

The motorcyclist turned his head to look at the books and then back to Jake. "I wouldn't be going into the forests around here these days."

"You're the second person who has said that to me. What gives? Bears? The vets? The Beast Man? The general spookiness of the woods?"

"I carried a heavy machine gun through the jungles of Nam for a year. I can deal with general spookiness.

"First," said the motorcyclist, holding up a chubby finger of one hand, "you've got the mushroom hunters who would just as soon slit your throat if you get too close to their secret stash, then," holding up a second finger, "you have the pot growers armed to keep you away from their plants, third," holding up another finger, "and yes, the vets who know a thing or two about guns.

"You have the Beast Man," holding up a fourth finger, "which I don't know is real or not, but lots of people believe in, and finally," flipping up a thick pinkie finger, "you have the crazy cults who practice god-knows-what deep in the forests.

"I'd rather drink beer at the Green Hornet than stick my nose in the woods these days."

Jake was about to ask who wouldn't rather drink beer at the Green Hornet when Bing raced into the office.

"Jake, Jake, you better come quick. There's a riot on the main street!"

CHAPTER 38

Jake had been to riots — windows smashed, cars set on fire, police firing tear gas canisters into crowds — and this wasn't a riot.

Still, it was a pretty ugly scene.

Twenty to thirty young guys in faded striped work shirts with their cuffs ripped off to prevent catches in machinery and rugged pants cut short over heavy laced-up boots had surrounded eight to 10 vets in their camo jackets and fatigues. The confrontation spilled off the sidewalk, stopping traffic throughout the town's main street. Horns were honking, and some drivers were egging the young men on.

The guys were yelling and cursing at the vets, and a couple brandished pick axes. Larry was one of the vets. He didn't look too concerned. They had likely trained for angry mobs.

After snapping off a few quick photos, Jake ran up to one of the young men standing back from the melee.

"What's happening?"

"It's these damn vets making the woods unsafe to work in. One of them shot at a logging truck yesterday. We want them gone, we want them out of here. Go back to Seattle where they came from!"

Jake figured the vets didn't necessarily come from Seattle, but logic was the first causality of a riot.

"How do you know it was a vet who shot at the truck?"

"Who else would it be? They are illegally camped all over out there. The Feds have made it almost impossible for a man to earn a paycheck, and now these yahoos are shooting at us. Get out of here, you bums!"

The last was yelled at the vets, not him, Jake hoped.

"Break it up! Break it up!" Sheriff Ramblewood had rolled up in her police car and waded into the men, her short size getting lost among the beefy timber workers. "Get back on the sidewalk. Go back to work. Leave these people alone."

Jake snapped off another quick photo, this one of the sheriff pushing into the chest of a bearded logger, his tin hat covering an unruly mass of hair, his face embarrassed at being confronted by the short female sheriff.

In a few minutes, the sheriff and several deputies separated the two groups, and the hot emotions dissipated. Traffic resumed on the main street, although a few male drivers still honked and gave a single-fingered salute to the vets as they drove past.

"I've called in the feds," the sheriff told Jake, lifting her voice to be heard by anyone within listening range. "They'll get to the bottom of the alleged shooting, as it happened on national forest land. Frankly, I don't even know if a shot was fired; I can't find anyone who was there. It could all be a baseless rumor. But, my job is to keep order in the county, which I will do." She raised her voice more for the last four words.

She turned away to speak to a couple of shop owners, and Jake drifted over to Larry.

"You OK?"

Larry gave Jake an "are you kidding me?" look.

"So, you're fine. Great. But this little mob scene is only the start if we don't get to the bottom of some of these mysteries. Lanie has to talk to the police about what she saw when Darrell was murdered. And vets who only want to live in peace and be left alone must help the police find the shooter."

"No one shot."

"No one shot? Do you mean no one shot at the logging truck? How can you be sure?"

Larry's eyes followed the other vets disappearing down the street, melting away among the tourists crowding along the storefronts.

"OK, you want to go, but you must talk with Lanie again. A half an hour, an hour with the sheriff, and maybe a solid lead to Darrell's murder could be uncovered. They could meet on neutral ground, like the tent behind the Sarge's house."

Larry gave an almost imperceptible nod, turned, and walked down an alley between two tourist stores. Soon, he was out of Jake's sight.

*****

Back at the office, Jake downloaded his photos. The one showing the small sheriff pushing back the manly logger was definitely page one.

Unless something new came along, and the way the news was breaking here in Pacific County, that was a good possibility.

"Jake, I'm worried about Bing's Bitches this week."

"Worried?" Jake had been worried since the column of rants and raves — actually, almost all rants — had begun. He was sure lawsuits would ensue.

Bing burst into laughter. "I'm worried it will be too fantastic! More calls are coming in every night. We have two feuds, with back-and-forth accusations, and this shooting of a logger by vets has inflamed people!"

"Wait, wait. A logger wasn't shot, just a logging truck shot at. We don't know if a vet was the shooter or even if there was a shot. Police are investigating."

"Pffft, facts," said Bing dismissively. "The best call that came in last night, though, was from a man claiming to be the Beast Man of the woods."

"What? Let's hear it."

"I thought you would say that." Bing hit the play button on the message machine.

"I called to say I am sorry," the soft male voice began. "I saw a prank on YouTube last year of some kids pretending to be a wild man in the woods, and I thought it would be fun to do that here. This town is so dull. I cut out some plywood footprints and made tracks around one of the cranberry bogs. Then, I called in a sighting. When that call was reported in the *Beachcomber*, I laughed and laughed. I made anonymous calls on other sightings, left footprints around the high school track — that got the girls' cheer team screaming — and talked up the Beast Man with my friends.

"Then I was stunned when other people started calling the sheriff's office with Beast Man sightings and blaming the Beast Man for stealing goats, taking food out of fridges in the garages, and wrecking gardens.

"And the *Beachcomber* printed it all. It's like you were in on it with me!

"But now it has gone too far. I'm afraid somebody will get shot due to hysteria over the Beast Man. One of my neighbors pulled a gun on another neighbor last night who was redelivering some mail that had been placed in the wrong mailbox.

"The *Beachcomber* helped me create this frenzy. Now, help me end it."

Bing hit the stop button.

"Wow," said Jake. "Play it again, there's something about the voice, but before you do, turn up the volume. What's with all the traffic noise in the background?"

"Sounds like it was made from a sidewalk pay phone."

"Pay phone? We don't have pay phones anymore."

"There's one right outside of Ruby's. It's part of her 1950's diner motif. Don't you pay attention to what's around you? Or do you just go there for the juicy pies and sexy waitress?"

CHAPTER 39

Well, Bing was correct — likely the first time Jake thought that in the weeks he had been at the *Beachcomber* — there was a pay phone in front of Ruby's.

He dropped a quarter into the coin slot and heard a familiar ding.

As a teenager, he wanted to call a girl for a first date but didn't want to use the family phone in the kitchen where his mom was making dinner. He walked down to a corner drugstore, entered the phone booth just inside the front door, and dropped in a dime, for which he got three nervous minutes of stammering and stuttering. When she said, "Yes," he was elated — a dime well spent.

The call from the Beast Man was made in the evening to the answering machine hooked up after hours at the newspaper to collect Bing's Bitches. Jake looked around. Who could have seen a caller?

"Hey, Ruby, did you see anyone using the pay phone last night?" She was at the cash register, adding up a tab, when he came in.

"Gosh, Jake, between serving diners here and dreaming about my favorite newspaperman, I don't have time to look outside." She smiled playfully, then went back to totaling the bill.

"OK, I know you are busy. But, surely, it must be unusual to see someone use the outside phone — young guy, old guy, tall, short, clean-shaven. Anything would help. How about anyone else here who was on shift last night?"

"I can ask."

"Or, does Ruby's have a surveillance camera pointed outside? Could I see the tape from last night?"

"Jake, we're not a bank or pawn shop. We're a pie shop. We don't care who is walking by, we only care if they come in and order a slice and a cup of joe."

"What are you looking for?" A man had pulled a credit card from his wallet and stood next to the cash register. "I have a camera pointed at the sidewalk. We've had some trouble in the past."

Jake turned to the man, who had tats up both arms, disappearing beneath the armholes of his muscle shirt, which carried the logo for Octopussy Tattoos.

Jake introduced himself and added, "The newspaper received a strange call last evening, I think from the pay phone outside, and I would like to see who made the call. Does your camera see the phone?"

"Not the phone itself. That's Ruby's area of the street. But if you know the time of the call, we could look to see who was walking on the street then, either coming to or leaving the phone. Unless they approached from the other direction, then we would have nothing."

Jake called Bing, got the time of the call, and followed the man — who had introduced himself as Curt, owner of Octopussy Tattoos — into his shop.

"Octopussy… that's an interesting name," Jake said, looking around at the designs on the walls evenly divided between scenes with large-breasted women and maritime motifs. Sometimes, the two overlapped.

"Yeah, that's what I thought. A little sex sells, even in tattoos. I worried the name might be a turnoff for women, but since most of them have a shot or two of tequila before coming in, they giggle at the play on words. And guys, of course, are dogs, and the name is a call whistle for them."

Pulling out a cell phone from under the counter, Curt tapped a few buttons, and the street scene appeared. "This app captures what the camera saw. Do you say about 7:30? Let me skip ahead, ah, here we are, 7 p.m. last night."

Curt sped up the playback. Jake was relieved to see only a few people walk by after store hours. Some couples, a few families with kids, a couple of solitary old guys, women in twos and threes... and then, about 7:40, a single guy looking like the dictionary definition of furtively, glancing rapidly left and right to see if anyone was looking at him.

Ahhh,... thought Jake. Now I recognize that voice.

"Thanks," Jake said to the tattoo shop owner. "I got what I needed. Anything I can do for you?"

"How about keeping my name out of the police blotter column?"

Jake laughed. "You know what the old-time politician said — 'I don't care what you print about me, just spell my name right.' He knew any publicity was good publicity. The police blotter might be a boon for business with a name like Octopussy."

Curt nodded, smiled, and handed Jake a business card showing a female-faced busty octopus squirting ink. "So that you get it right."

*****

"Hey, Jake, you came to tell me the *Beachcomber* wants to publish one of my sci-fi novels after all?"

"No, Levi, that's not why I am here. I came to talk about the phone call last night."

"Oh." Levi's face fell. He turned his head slightly to the side, where he could see his mom busy in the kitchen. "Hey, mom, this is the editor of the newspaper. We're going downstairs to my room to discuss some of my ideas."

To Jake, he tilted his head towards an open door with stairs leading down.

"How did you figure out it was me?"

Jake knew the question would be coming, so he had run through several answers and approaches to take. He could get all angry about the fear caused, go schoolmarm stern about misbehaving, or even offer congratulations on punking the town.

Ultimately, he had decided a simple story puncturing the Beast Man myth was the best.

"It had to be somebody with imagination, and you have imagination to the moon and back," he began, playing to the boy's ego. "Start from the beginning. But, this has to be on the record, so let me make some notes."

Levi eyed the reporter's notebook in Jake's hands, sighed deeply, and began talking, filling in details from the basic story he had told on the phone.

"What will I do, Jake, when everybody reads it was me behind the Beast Man? Will I have to leave town? Will my mother be in danger?"

"Levi, I cannot predict what will happen. Yes, likely, some people will say something. You will get some dark looks. Maybe a few people will stop speaking to you. But I doubt a mob will show up with pitchforks and torches.

"And, who knows, some kids your age will admire you and the prank you pulled. You'll probably make new friends out of all of this."

"New friends…?" The downcast Levi started seeing the sun break through the clouds of regret for the Beast Man events that led to the phone call.

By the time he saw Jake off at the front door, he was back to his optimistic self.

"Hey, I have an idea — I could write a book called *I Was the Beast Man of Long Beach.* Cool, huh?"

Now was the time for the stern schoolmarm glare from Jake.

But in truth, he thought, walking back to the office, it probably would be a best seller for the *Beachcomber.*

CHAPTER 40

"John Ryan, this could be the week for the talking dolphin story. Our top story is the Beast Man unmasked. A cuddly animal story would be perfect for the bottom of the front page."

"You are so right, Jake." John had come in Friday afternoon to pick up his paycheck, which Jake was glad to see Bing hand him without comment.

"But I think our little outing to the autopsy Saturday will be explosive... we should save the talking dolphin for a slow news week. She says she's not going anywhere."

The words "slow news week" made Jake realize that the *Beachcomber* hadn't had a slow news week since he had been there. Between the mysterious mill fire and as yet the unidentified body found, the murder of the cranberry grower, the continuing uncertainties over the bodies in the freezers, the baffling killing of the former publishers, and the heightened frictions between town people and the homeless vets, the reporting staff had been run ragged trying to keep up.

It could make an editor wish for a slow news week, except not. A good newspaper is all about what's new. When there's nothing new, what's the point of a newspaper?

"So what is this autopsy story?"

"I don't want to give too much away, Jake, this is one of those stories best if you don't know much going in. I want to see your honest reactions. I'll be by about 3 to 4 Saturday to pick you up.

"But now, I'm off to see a woman."

"A woman? The talking dolphin?"

"No, Jake. Maybe the perfect woman for me, smart, attractive, athletic, outgoing, a success in her own right... and she's buying dinner."

"I didn't know you were dating, John. Anyone I know?"

"She's not from the Green Hornet if that's what you mean. And sure, I'm dating. A man doesn't get married four times by sitting on his thumbs."

*****

"I haven't seen anything more in the paper about those bodies in the freezers."

The question from Ruby made Jake's heart quicken. He enjoyed a woman who read his newspaper. Or maybe it was the second mile of walking in the sand along the longest beach in the world — as the town of Long Beach insisted.

They had driven 10 miles north of Long Beach to find a deserted stretch of ocean for their walk. Once past the deep dry sand and driftwood along the shore, they had found firmer footing in the wet sand at the ocean's edge.

When the long waves swept the beach, bubbles popped up from what Jake guessed were wormholes. Even though it was Friday afternoon, only a few other beach walkers were out.

"I think those bodies have something to do with the story John Ryan and I are covering tomorrow. Say, did you know John was dating? Sounds serious, too."

"Yes, he was in the diner a couple of days ago with a woman. He was talking, waving around his hands, and she was laughing. It looked like a date."

"So, is this a date we are on, a long romantic walk on a practically deserted beach?" Out here, in an open nature wonderland where he could see for miles, his suspicions of Ruby dissipated like the mist in the distance. He remembered the warmth she was bringing into his life.

"Why not?" She wrapped an arm inside his and snuggled up to his side, her red hair blowing in the ocean breeze.

"You know, I've enjoyed our time together, despite the odd way we met. It's like a 'cute meet' in a chick flick that turns into something special. I don't care what you've done in the past or may have had to do to survive, I see you for who you are today, and I'm falling for that person."

She abruptly stopped and pulled back from Jake.

"And just what do you think I had to do to survive in the past?"

"Well, huh... I don't know, but there was that guy at the gas station... he acted as if he owned you."

"So, a stranger at a gas station shouts something, and you color in a disreputable past for me?"

"Well, that," and Jake knew he was digging the hole deeper but couldn't stop talking, "and the easy way you came into my bed that first night."

"The easy way I came into your bed made you what? Think I was a pro at what, working the sheets?"

Ruby backed up further from Jake. His brain was screaming to shut up and apologize, but his mouth wasn't listening.

"I said I don't care what you once were or once did. I'm all for just going on from here. You seem like the perfect woman for me, and I want to be with you."

"Oh, how big of you. Willing to forgive my disreputable past if I — a reformed whatever — will stay in your bed now."

She turned and angrily stomped off. Jake watched the single line of footprints in the sand grow in the distance between them.

With a heavy heart, he followed them to the car for the frosty ride home.

CHAPTER 41

Ruby stayed in the RV Friday night after the argument on the beach and shared the bed with Jake. But there weren't any friendly touching or soothing words from her.

Jake piddled around the *Beachcomber* Saturday, trying to write an editorial for the next week's edition. All he got was a few paragraphs contemplating the mysteries of a woman's mind. Probably not a good opinion piece for a community newspaper.

When Ruby left for her shift starting at noon, he returned to the RV to make himself a light lunch. What was the proper meal before an autopsy, he wondered.

At 4, John Ryan knocked on the door.

"Got your black clothes on, 'cause we're heading to an autopsy."

"I got my black mood on," replied a sour Jake.

"Sounds like woman troubles. I know about those four or five times over. This will give you something else to think about. I'll write the main story, but I want you there when trouble breaks out."

"Trouble?"

"Yeah, we may not have revealed our full identities when I bought the tickets from a guy who needed a few extra bucks. You can reimburse me later."

*****

The parking lot around the two-story metal industrial building in the Port's business campus was jammed when John and Jake pulled up in Jake's pickup.

John had said to keep a low profile, so Jake parked well away from the front door and backed into a slot, just in case a quick getaway should be necessary.

There was something off about the other vehicles, and it took a moment for Jake to realize what it was — most of them were BMWs or other higher-end cars and pickups — not vehicles with rust holes from the salt water typically seen around Long Beach. Checking out the advertising frames around the license plates, all were from dealers closer to Seattle.

"This looks like a black-tie affair," said Jake, quietly closing his door not to attract attention. "What did these tickets cost, anyway?"

"$500." John joined Jake as the two casually walked towards a front door.

"$500? Wow!"

"Each."

"Each? The newspaper can't reimburse you for that!"

John dismissed Jake's comment with a wave of his hand. "Think of all the extra papers we're going to sell."

"John, we don't sell that many papers on the newsstands each week... maybe 250 to 300. We'd have to print and sell another 1,000 to pay for these tickets."

"Jake, this is going to be a great story, it might make your career, even though you are just helping me. Quit thinking like an accountant and think like what you are in the blood: an ink slinger with a massive story to tell."

By now, the two had approached the front door, where a doorman was collecting tickets. Jake had worn a baseball cap and kept his head low but noticed that none of the others lining up at the door were making eye contact either. Like Jake, they were all trying to appear invisible. Yet, an audible hum of anticipation flowed through the air.

The gruff-faced man at the door took the two tickets John handed over, then held his challenging gaze, first on John and then Jake. What if he doesn't let us in, and the newspaper is out $1,000, worried Jake. But after a long minute, the doorman tore the tickets in half, handed back the stubs, and tilted his head towards the door.

Once inside, the scene reminded Jake of a Hollywood game show filming. Risers with seating for a couple of hundred rose on one dark side. A stage lit by bright lights took up about a third of the remaining floor space, TV cameras patrolled the stage's rim, and chairs for the director and crew took up the rest of the room. Monitors were mounted above the scene to provide good views of what the cameras were seeing.

All that was missing was a flashing applause sign.

The stage was set up to look like an operating room — machines displaying flashing readouts, tubes and IVs hanging from stands, a gurney in the middle, and a green sheet draped over something on the gurney.

When Jake shot a questioning glance at John, he replied, "I told you it would be televised. Let's sit at the far end to watch the audience and the stage."

They had hardly taken their seats when a man in a shiny green suit jumped on stage and started addressing the audience, which, in looking around, Jake saw was primarily male.

"Good evening! Great to see you here! We have a fabulous show for you tonight!"

The audience broke into applause. Maybe there was an applause sign, after all, thought Jake.

The man dropped his voice and leaned toward the audience in a co-conspirator manner. "Look, there are some things we don't do in modern society. We are so wrapped up in plastic cubicles, sanitized, and fed 'safe' versions of life that we don't see the real. Our hunters and gatherer ancestors — especially the hunters," the man paused to smile and allow the audience to break into applause again, "knew what is kept at a distance from us today.

"We walk around in our bodies every day. But what do we know about the machinery that runs our bodies? We might see pretty colored drawings of a human body when we go to a doctor's office, but I can tell you, those drawings are for children.

You are not children, are you?"

"No!" came the chorus of a reply.

"Television shows like CSI with their autopsy scenes have whetted the appetite for viewers to see the amazing machinery inside the human body, but those shows are so fake."

A smattering of boos and hisses broke out.

"Tonight, here, on stage, right in front of you, we have natural human bodies, an actual doctor, a real knife, and what he will pull out of those bodies will be more real than anything you have ever seen in your lives!

"Dr. Gregory, if you please!"

A tall man in green hospital scrubs and a surgical mask walked on stage to applause, which he soon quieted when he swept the audience with a look of serious demeanor.

A shapely blonde assistant in tight scrubs and a mask swept the sheet from the gurney, and there was a naked woman's body, caught on two cameras for the monitors: one camera showing the scene on the stage, another directly overhead on just the body.

"What the hell!" Jake muttered, joining a general chorus of amazement from around him. His hands gripped the riser seat, where he realized a small paper bag was taped — a bag like those on airplanes for air-sick-prone passengers.

"First, we cut...." When Dr. Gregory brought the knife down on the woman's chest, Jake jumped up and quickly stepped to the side where the stage was not visible.

"Your first autopsy?" The man in the green suit took his eyes off the stage and handed Jake a paper bag. "You might need this."

Taking the bag just in case, Jake asked, "Is this legal?"

"Well, it is not illegal. Not in this state."

"You can just cut up bodies? For a TV show?"

"We call it educational TV. Exactly why people watch is not our concern. For some, it's a learning experience, sure. Still, for others..." he nodded towards the audience where subdued light caught the men uniformly leaning forward, eyes glued to the stage, something between a look of wonder and the look of a predator on their faces. Hungry wolves are the image that flashed through Jake's mind.

"When we removed the intestines...." Jake caught a glimpse of Dr. Gregory pulling out the colon hand over hand and passing it off to his lovely assistant.

He yanked his eyes away from the monitor. "How many of these will you do tonight?"

"Three. The young woman there, an older woman — women are the most popular subjects — and one young boy, where everything is there, but at a much smaller scale."

"How do you get the bodies? You don't...." Jake thought of the beefy, unpleasant man at the door.

"No, no. These bodies all came to us already dead. Ha, ha, I've had others ask that question. We are not murderers. This is mostly a legal business. Although, to be honest, a few dollars might change hands when we get the bodies from mortuaries. Maybe the families believe they are getting their loved ones' ashes. There are always extra ashes lying around at a crematorium."

Jake's stomach settled as he found familiar footing asking questions of a source.

"Why Long Beach for your studio? And while tickets are expensive, do they pay for your costs? All these cameras, stage, and crew look expensive."

"Cheap rent and sparse police presence are the reasons for locating here. Plus, I like clam digging on the beach. And the audience, that's just for show. The real money comes from TV. We're on one of those premium channels you've never heard of, but people who like this kind of thing know well.

"This is," and the man bent into Jake's ear, "a high-profit business with an endless supply of products and little price resistance from buyers.

"I am looking for someone to help with logistics, though. We had some trouble a few weeks ago with transport. You seem interested and reasonably intelligent, looking to get into a fast-expanding enterprise where you can write your own ticket?"

"I already have a job. I'm the editor of the local paper." Jake pulled out a notebook and asked: "What did you say your name was?"

"A reporter? We don't allow reporters here!"

At the sound of "reporter," several men closest to Jake jumped up and started scurrying for the far side door where they had come in. In seconds, more joined them in the scramble.

"Dimitri, Dimitri," the man shouted over the erupting commotion. "Come quick!"

"Time for us to leave, partner." John Ryan grabbed Jake by the shoulder. "I saw a back door behind those curtains."

Jake and John pushed past the man in the green suit towards the door as Dr. Gregory carried on. "To remove the eyeball, I make a small cut just above the eyelid...."

The parking lot was a wild free-for-all, expensive cars peeling out, some banging into each other, but no one stopping to assess damages or exchange insurance information.

"This way," John pulled Jake towards swamp reeds growing at the edge of the pavement. "There is a back trail to town."

Jake could barely keep his footing, trotting quickly through the mud and guck, trying to keep up with a man 35 years his senior.

"Ah, listen, the music of the Moors. That's the old Wiggins' mansion, the third house that's fallen to Moroccan Law," said John as the pair wound past a large home. "That story just keeps on giving."

Soon the pair broke through the reeds into a parking lot behind the downtown commercial strip. They slowed their trot to a walk while catching their breaths.

"So that's what the bodies in the freezers were all about. What a story for this edition!" Jake was already playing with front page layouts in his mind. Would the Beast Man be the top story or the TV autopsies be the top? And where would the update on the McKinneys go? What if Pat got an update on the cranberry murder story? How could he fit everything?

"What's that flickering light? It looks like a fire!" John pointed farther down through town. "It's coming from around the *Beachcomber's* office."

CHAPTER 42

"Where's Ruby? Is she inside!"

"We thought both of you were inside when we got here," yelled a man in a yellow fire helmet over a raging fire ripping through the Hulk.

"Jake! Jake, I'm here. I'm OK." Ruby, wrapped in a blanket with Long Beach Fire Department stenciled on the black, reached out to wrap her arms around Jake's waist.

"What happened?" Jake returned the embrace. "Are you OK? Were you inside? Was it an accident?"

"It wasn't an accident," said the man in the helmet Jake recognized as Chief Smoke, the one paid employee of the otherwise all-volunteer department. "There was a strong odor of gasoline when we arrived, like somebody threw gas on the side of the RV and lit it. She was lucky to make it out."

Chief Smoke fixed his eyes on Jake. "The sheriff will want to ask you some questions when she arrives."

"Me?"

"When there is an arson fire of an abode, usually the perpetrator has a motive beyond just seeing flames. Especially when there is a relationship with whoever is inside."

He nodded at Ruby. "Good night, miss." Turning towards Jake, he added, "And you, don't go too far away."

By now, the flames had died out, partially from the water pumped on the rig but mainly because the fuel for the fire had been exhausted. Acidic smoke rose from a 30-foot sheet of charcoal, covering the engine and transmission on the asphalt like a wet quilt.

"Oh, Ruby, I've been so dumb." Jake laid his head on her

blanketed shoulder.

"You didn't start the fire?" She jerked back a foot to look into his face.

"No, no, of course not. I was running down the bodies in the freezers story with John Ryan. We first saw the fire from the other end of town.

"No, I've been dumb because I've had some weird thoughts about you — troubling ideas involving Big Red's treasure and why you were with me. I thought maybe you were using me to get the treasure for yourself.

"But when I saw the flames consuming the Hulk and thought you were inside... I wanted to run in and save you. And then when you called out my name, I knew... I knew I didn't care about the treasure near as much as I cared about you. If you want to use me to find the treasure, fine, just let me spend more time with you. Please."

"Oh, Jake, Jake." She wrapped her arms around him and squeezed. Pulling back, she smiled. "Aren't you a newsman? You're supposed to photograph other people running into fires to save women and children, not run in yourself, you big dummy."

People in the crowd of spectators started drifting off as the last flames died, leaving Jake and Ruby standing alone in the darkening parking lot.

"I do need to tell you something. I am not who you think I am. But that doesn't mean I'm an angel, either."

She swept the fire department blanket from her shoulders, folded it in half, and then half again and again. She then walked it over to the last aid vehicle, handing it to a volunteer firefighter who was packing up and preparing to leave.

Returning to Jake's side, she took a deep breath, looked once at him, and then out into the night.

"OK, so here goes. I'm a card counter, and the guy you saw at the gas station in Portland is... was my assistant."

"A card counter? I don't get it."

Ruby took another deep breath and then coughed a

couple of times from the fumes.

"Do you ever go to casinos and gamble on card games, like blackjack?"

"No. I've lost money on penny slots. Does that count?"

"OK, from the beginning. Cards that come up at casino games are seemingly random. Maybe your card comes up, and you win, or perhaps it doesn't, and the casino wins. The dealers at casinos are professionals. The customers are not. And often, they have a few free drinks in them. So even though sometimes the customers hit it big, the casinos know play enough hands, and the money flows towards the house.

"What I do..." she looked back at Jake, "my brain works in a funny way. I see the cards played at a table playing 21, and I can see which cards have been played and which are still in the unplayed stack.

"Even playing with five decks, as many casinos do, I know if, say, a majority of face cards have been played, then low cards are more likely to come up.

"Casinos don't like people like me. So, I use a ruse. I have an assistant — like the guy at the gas station — do the actual playing while I act up as the girlfriend on his shoulder. I might complain about being bored, wanting to return to the room, or wanting another drink when I subtly give him clues on how to bet.

"Sometimes we win, and sometimes we don't. But I'm good enough that money flows our way over enough hands rather than to the casinos."

Jake looked perplexed. "I knew you were smart, but I have never heard of outsmarting the casinos."

"Yeah, well, the casinos don't like it. So I have to trade out assistants often. The casinos closely monitor the player, not so much the crappy girlfriend on his shoulder."

"I wouldn't say crappy. You're beautiful. And, thankfully, alive."

"I wear a lot of cheap makeup, and the acting courses at the University of Washington help. I was hoping to be an actress until I discovered my true talent.

"The guy you saw in Portland? He was my last assistant. I guess I was firing him. He didn't take it so well. He probably didn't like that I held back his last couple of paydays, either."

"You think he did this?" Jake looked at the smoldering heap.

"Yes, I do. But let me make a phone call. If I promise the right people to stay out of casinos, they will take care of this problem for us."

"Take care...?"

"Ummm, don't think too much about it. In the meantime, where are we going to stay tonight?"

CHAPTER 43

It occurred to Jake as he was carrying an armful of shirts, pants, and underwear towards the front counter of Norma's Fashions that between replacing his wardrobe because of the fire, buying hiking boots at Goodwill and rain jackets at Garrett's Hardware, he was spending more money on clothes than he was earning at the *Beachcomber*.

He needed to nudge newspaper broker Dave Raymond again. Or get serious about looking for Big Red's treasure. And this time, Ruby would be his co-conspirator.

"What's new on the cranberry murder?" A 60-ish woman with thin, ratted, dyed pale blonde hair and sparkly strawberry lip gloss wearing a name tag "Norma" on a flowered smock was ringing up his sales. Fashion had left this station some time ago.

"We have a story this week with startling new revelations."

"Well, everyone is saying the coach didn't do it. I guess one of the vets was a girlfriend to Darrell. I bet she did it. Those people are crazy. I don't know why they let those people hang around."

"Maybe because they served their country?" Jake lifted two stuffed bags of clothes from the counter to leave.

"Humph. Other people have served their country and then come back to productive lives. A few years in the Army shouldn't earn you a lifetime of free handouts."

Jake saw no point in arguing. Besides, was Norma's Fashions an advertiser? He should ask Adele.

*****

The first stop was a little cabin from the 1940s behind Ruby's Diner.

The cabin, part of an old motor court, was one of eight in a tight horseshoe. Initially, each had a little covered adjacent parking area between cabins, but that area had been converted to paid storage when it became apparent the slots were too small for modern cars in the 1960s. Cars had gotten smaller again, but paid storage remained as it was a cash cow.

Amber, the owner of Ruby's, had offered the cabin to Jake and Ruby when she learned of the fire at the RV. An independent woman in her 70s, she had taken a liking to Ruby and was teaching her how to make pies and run a restaurant business.

Ruby returned the budding friendship, enjoying working in a legitimate enterprise where she got to use her talent for numbers for good.

Jake hung a few of his new shirts in the tiny closet. People traveled with fewer clothes in the 1940s.

One drawer in the small dresser took care of his pants and underwear. Owning fewer items sure uncomplicated life, but Jake wondered how much more uncomplicated he wanted his life to get.

He was down to not much than the material on his back, his aging Tacoma pickup, and a dwindling bank account. Were it not for good luck in collecting a finder's fee for lost gold treasure in Arizona, he would be homeless and broke — like those vets.

But he had a job and a girl. Or, woman, actually. Of the two, the woman paid the most benefits but was also the most uncertain. The night of the fire, he had told Ruby he would quit doubting her, but those suspicions lingered in his mind.

The old Kenny Roger's song drifted through his mind: 'Oh, Ruby, don't take your love to town....''

The Ruby in the song was playing false with her husband, a dying Vietnam veteran. How about this Ruby? Was she playing false with Jake? Was her love for the bootlegger's money and not Jake? Would she take her love somewhere else when his usefulness was gone?

CHAPTER 44

"Sheriff, you look a little under the weather today."

"Hi, Jake. It's this job. You see the worst in people, even those who you love."

Jake slid into a bench seat across the table from the sheriff having coffee, picking idly at Marionberry pie at Ruby's Diner.

"I've heard that comment more than once when covering the cops beat for the *Seattle Times*. But in a big city, I would guess, it's a little less personal. Here, I imagine you know just about everyone or their families."

Sheriff Ramblewood took a deep breath and, holding a bite of pie on a fork, looked carefully at Jake while making up her mind about something.

"You did us — and the town — a huge favor by unmasking the Beast Man. And the witness to Darrell's murder came in and talked with us yesterday, so it looks like you won't be moving into one of my cells. Although maybe you want the protection after the RV fire?"

"No, I'm good. I think we can take care of that problem. So, what's weighing on you?"

"It's Darrell's murder." She took another deep breath. "As I told you, he and the track coach had a business enterprise that didn't go well. Looking through Darrell's business files, we found some things that... well... don't reflect so great on him."

"Like what?" Jake silently pointed to the sheriff's pie while catching the eye of Ruby behind the counter. Pie for breakfast always brightened his day.

"He and the coach did have a little business. They were

working on ideas for making cranberries into a dried snack to be sold to moms preparing lunches for kids. I guess done right, dried cranberries are high in antioxidants or something. But they never got the drying process down before they ran out of the coach's money.

"Anyway, looking through Darrell's farm operation records, we found evidence he was selling cranberries to his son, Bobby."

"Yeah...?"

"And then, Bobby was reselling them at farmers' markets as organic berries when they definitely were not organic."

"Ohhh... That doesn't sound very ethical, although I've always thought what sellers said at unregulated markets, like roadside stands and farmers' markets, was full of puffery. I thought that was a gray area in the law."

"Two things. First, Darrell was leading the charge against the claims of the organic cranberry growers. Being a history buff, he knew the crops were almost wiped out 100 years ago and were only saved by chemical sprays.

"It looks like while he was loudly defending the modern practices of growers, he was also feeding berries to the organic competition for a profit. And this public feud with his son was a way of covering up their dealings."

"Oh, and I had always heard great things about Darrell. Still, in my reporting, I have too often discovered the biggest talkers about righteousness can also be the biggest sinners."

"Yeah, just lying to the community and friends is one thing. Not really in my action area.

"But, Darrell's records — and he was a methodical record keeper — showed he was covering up the sales of berries to Bobby by claiming he was losing berries to cranberry rustlers."

"Oh my god!"

"When we went back to look at reported incidents of cranberry rustling, we found Darrell was the first to report it and the most frequent."

"Sheriff, I need to report this. Cranberry rustling has caused a lot of fear in the community. Let me make some notes."

"I know who I am talking to. Make your notes. Because it gets worse."

After another heavy breath, the sheriff continued. "Growing cranberries using organic methods is not too successful. Or, at least Bobby and the other organic growers never found the proper techniques because while they had an eager and growing market, they didn't have the berries.

"Darrell couldn't keep up with demand, so he brought some friends into the scheme. Other growers started reporting rustling while clandestinely feeding berries to the organic market."

"I don't get it. The growers own their crops. Besides the obvious problem of selling non-organic berries as organic, why report the diversion as thefts?"

"All the non-organic growers sell their berries to Ocean Spray. Ocean Spray works hand-in-glove with growers, often providing crop financing, so they keep a tight focus on the expected harvest. If production unexpectedly dips, they want to know why. The rustling claims were a way to get around them.

"OK, I can see that."

"Now we come to the part that breaks my heart." The sheriff laid down her fork and turned her head away from Jake to look outside.

"Darrell was always my favorite uncle. As a kid, I loved playing on the old tractors he had in his museum. As a teenager, I helped with the harvest, earning fun money. He was there the night I got crowned Miss Cranberry, and, as I have said, he was the one who urged me to run when the previous sheriff got caught with his pants down.

"He was my biggest fan, always a smile, always saying, 'Great job, girl!'"

Was that a tear starting down the cheek of the sheriff? Jake had seen cops cry. In some ways, cops have the softest hearts, but maybe that's because they see the most terrible things.

"But along with everything else, the double dealings, the false reports, the lying, Darrell was reporting the thefts to his insurance company.

"He was collecting insurance money on the thefts he was doing himself."

*****

"Then who did kill the dishonest cranberry grower?" Ruby had refilled Jake's cup as he completed his notes from the interview with the sheriff and slid into the bench seat Sheriff Ramblewood had recently vacated. "Anything new on that? The coach? The coach's wife? Another grower?"

"The sheriff said because of Lanie's eyewitness account, they had given up on thinking the killer was the track coach, who is a tall, thin man, a typical runner's profile. They now think the killer was a shorter person, five-three, five-four, more like your height."

"I'm five-five-and-a-half if you please. Well, I didn't kill him."

Jake quickly looked up, seeing Ruby in a fresh light. He had never entertained the idea she might have killed Darrell, but could she have? Why? Once an idea is in the brain, it's hard to unthink it… and to stop the brain from firing off synapses, connecting one idea with another.

"Something else, the sheriff said in passing. In the back of one of Darrell's file cases, behind the usual business stuff, was a folder with just a couple of sheets of paper. On one paper was writing, but not in English."

"Maybe it was some foreign business contact, like with France. They like garnishes and flavorings. Maybe they are into cranberries."

"No, this was in a different alphabet. More of a rugged script."

"Huh. Did she leave the folder in Darrell's office?"

"She didn't say. She did say in the folder was an old map. Why?"

Ruby shrugged. "Who knows where the next clue to the bootlegger's fortune will come from? We need to see that file and map, Jake!"

"I think we should work on what we have," he said, quietly thinking he should learn more about the file before sharing information with Ruby. "As the old farmer said, 'it's hard to plow a straight furrow when you're moving your eyes all around.'"

"Yes," countered Ruby, "but, 'It's the wandering dog that finds the bone.'"

They both laughed, and Jake relaxed. Being with a woman who enjoyed mental bantering was a playful delight.

*****

"My lunch break is coming up," she said, cleaning the coffee cups from the diner's table.

"Oh... time enough for a dessert dish of afternoon delight?"

She smiled but shook her head slowly. "Time enough to run out to Darrell's and look for that file. Ten minutes there, 10 minutes back, and 40 minutes of sleuthing. Let's go."

Yellow police tape sagged at the barn's entrance at Darrell Green's cranberry operation. The sliding front door was already slightly open, revealing a sliver of darkness on the other side.

Jake pulled out his iPhone and turned on the flashlight. "Into the dark unknown, we go. Who knows what mysteries lurk." His attempt at sounding dramatic fell on deaf ears as Ruby pushed past.

She suddenly stopped. "What was that? Did you see the light on the other side of that old tractor?"

"No. Maybe it was your eyes getting used to the dark. Here, follow me. I bet his office is at the back, beyond the tractors and antique farming machinery."

"Ow, damnit, Jake! Keep your light down here, not looking at the old cranberry harvest photos on the walls. I walked into a wheelbarrow. And, are you sensing we are not alone?"

"Darrell's ghost?" By now, the light of day had faded, and the dark windows added to the spookiness of the barn outfitted as a museum.

Reaching the back of the barn, the pair came to Darrell's office. Jake tried the door, and the knob turned easily.

"Oh, good," he said, shining his light around the small office. "He only had one file cabinet." Pulling open the top drawer, they rifled through tabbed files and saw each labeled as tax records from different years.

Working their way to the bottom drawer, they found what they sought. "Look!" said Ruby, kneeling beside the cabinet. She pulled the file from the back, which fell open to show a hand-drawn map. "This is different from Jane's map!"

"Leave that right there!" ordered a voice from the dark office doorway.

Jake and Ruby jerked their heads around, their eyes caught in a laser-bright beam. All they could see at the edge of the shaft was a hand holding a pistol aimed right at them. The speaker's face was hidden in the dark.

"Get out of here!" The speaker — and the light and gun — slide to the side, opening a path out of the door. "And don't look at me!"

Ruby sprung up, and she and Jake hustled out the door and through the barn.

"Who was that?" she asked in a hushed voice. "It sounded like a woman."

"Maybe Darrell's murderer, coming back, looking for the file we found. Get to the pickup, we don't want to end up like Darrell." Jake fished his keys from his pocket.

"Wait. Get the pickup started, but let's wait to see who comes out."

"Ruby, I don't want to be shot at. And it's getting too dark to see."

"OK, get turned around, but don't go yet."

She kept her eyes on the barn door, where a small figure emerged after several seconds, face covered in a hoodie.

CHAPTER 45

Another week's paper was out, and Jake found his favorite stool at the Green Hornet, breathing a sigh of relief after the scary encounter at Darrell's barn — and pride of accomplishment in his newspaper work.

Jake didn't know how he had done it, fitting the breaking news of the bodies in the freezer, Darrel's double dealings, and the Russian connection to the McKinney's deaths — on the front page, but he had, along with a photo from the fire that destroyed the Hulk.

The great American wit Will Rogers once said, 'It ain't bragging if you've done it." It wasn't bragging to be proud of his work this week.

He felt pretty good as he lifted a can of Mr. Sun, a hazy pale ale with a drawing of a lumberjack looking over a forest from Fremont Brewing in Seattle. He felt like a lumberjack, having cut through a forest of distractions this week to put out perhaps the best issue of the *Beachcomber* in years. If not ever.

"Well, mate, you made a dog's breakfast out of that one. I would have figured the rain would have run you off by now."

"Oh, hi. I shouldn't be surprised to see an Aussie at a bar."

"It is our natural habitat, all right. You get the first one, and I'll get the second."

Jake was about to say he was already on the first beer, but what the hell? It had been a world-beater week. And, maybe the Australian had a story for next week, as he had made a point to take the next stool to Jake.

"Jake, Jake, come quick! John Ryan has been shot at his

desk!" Bing was at the tavern door, her head and shoulders inside, but her feet rooted outside as if she was afraid of being seen in the bar — or had once been banned. Either could be true, Jake figured as he popped off the stool, trying to make sense of her words. Who would shoot John Ryan? And what was John doing at the office on a Wednesday night?

"Set one up for my mate here," said Jake, leaving a $5 bill on the bar, "I got to bail."

Velma didn't look pleased to be left alone with the Aussie.

*****

Flashing lights from emergency vehicles once again filled the *Beachcomber's* parking lot. An ambulance with open back doors was parked over the scorched spot in the asphalt where the Hulk had burned just a few days ago.

"What happened? Who shot him?" Jake had asked Bing in the fast trot from the Green Hornet to the newspaper.

"I don't know! I had dropped by to make sure the message machine was on and working — we are getting so many calls to Bing's Bitches, I really should get a raise for coming up with that idea, by the way — and John was at his desk, typing. Weird he was working on a Wednesday evening.

"Anyway, as I bent over the phone on my desk, I heard a bang! And the sound of John falling into his desk. I turned as he rolled onto the floor, blood spurting from his chest!"

"Did you see who did it?"

"The shot came through the window. When I could get my eyes off John, whoever shot him was gone."

Jake pushed past EMTs at the office door, reaching the inert John Ryan being lifted onto a gurney. Emergency bandages covering his right shoulder were turning a deep red.

"John, John, are you all right?"

"Jake…" came a weak reply.

"Stand back! We got to get him out of here." An ETM

pushed Jake in the chest out of the way.

"How serious is it?"

"An upper body wound. We won't know until we get him to the hospital. Now, clear away!"

"Jake... it's all connected... it's all connected." John's voice grew weaker as the gurney rolled past towards the ambulance.

"What does he mean?" Bing had come up to Jake, the excitement of a spectator at a crime scene in her voice.

"I have no idea. What was he working on?"

"He didn't say a word to me when I came in, he was so focused on typing."

John's computer screen had timed out to black. The keyboard — knocked to the floor by his fall — was covered in blood but still connected to the computer.

Jake knelt on one knee and directed a pointer finger at one of the few unbloodied keys to bring the screen back to life.

"Stop! That's a crime scene. Step away, Jake." Sheriff Ramblewood clutched his shoulder and pulled back.

"Sheriff, I wanted to see what he was working on. Maybe it's a clue... maybe it was the reason he was shot." Or, thought Jake, maybe it was finally the talking dolphin story.

"Wait! Let me do it." The sheriff pulled on a plastic glove and tapped a key, lighting up the screen.

The three — the sheriff, Jake, and Bing — peered at the words on the screen.

"A three-month-long investigation by this reporter has revealed a link between local murders and mayhem with deep roots in the history of our community.

"This link has drawn in hardcore criminals from the outside and corrupted local citizens of good standing.

"This link is placing innocent local residents in danger while feeding fears that have divided our town...."

"Good lord, John, get to the point!" Jake nearly shouted as both an editor and a reader sucked in by the promise of a great story.

But the words on the screen stopped.

"You're his editor," said the sheriff turning to Jake. "What's he talking about?"

"I don't know. Honestly, I don't know. He is working on a few stories, but nothing like this, at least, not that he told me."

"We will have to take the computer and keyboard in as evidence. Can you help me pack it up?"

"Sheriff, come on. We have only three news computers, and I don't want to give up one. Who knows when we might get it back? I want to get to the bottom of John's shooting as much as you — maybe more. Let me read his files. I can make a copy for you or send you anything I find suspicious. The *Beachcomber* is running on fumes… we can't afford to buy a new computer."

The sheriff took a moment, looked around the anything-but-flashy office, and said, "OK, get me a copy of all his files tonight. With passwords."

Bing edged closer to Jake. "Am I in danger, too? Maybe I was the target. Our backs were turned to the windows, maybe the shooter made a mistake. You know Bing's Bitches has generated a lot of heat."

"Bing. I think you are safe. No one will mistake the back of a 70-year-old man with…" Jake paused to find the politically correct words for a woman with a well-padded backside, "your youthful air."

"Yes, you are right. John Ryan was an old, old man. Hey, will you take any crime scene photos for next week's paper? Want me in them to express shock and horror as a near victim?"

CHAPTER 46

"What did John Ryan mean when he said, 'It's all connected'…?"

Ruby was propped up on the double-wide bed, one leg drawn up, phone in her hand, dressed for a mid-morning shift at the diner.

"I have no idea. As far as I know, John was working on three stories: the company doing the televised autopsies, the Moorish takeover of local homes, and a talking dolphin. I could not imagine a more diverse set of stories… they could not possibly be connected."

Jake lounged in an overstuffed armchair from the mid-last century, a pole lamp next to him and a doily-covered tiny circular table on the other side. A very comfortable arrangement, he had decided.

While the cabin was tiny by any standards, it was more spacious than the living space in the Hulk. Jake felt like he could spread out. He idly wondered how long they could stay in the old motor court cabin owned by Ruby's boss at the diner.

"When are you going to talk to John to find out?"

"I'm told he has been transferred to a hospital in Longview. I planned on driving down today."

"I wish I could go with you, but I don't want to duck out on Amber, especially now she is letting us live here for free."

"You'd be great company." Jake was glad Ruby was not coming with him, as he was looking forward to talking to John alone.

"I'm brought up this map of Big Red's homes. And then I looked at John's story about the Moors. Here, notice anything?"

She held out her phone to show Jake the map photo.

"OK," said Jake, standing from his chair to look at the phone. Was this symbolic in their relationship that he was going more than halfway to meet her? Jake put that thought away. "It's too small to see. Tell me what you see, as you've been studying that map a lot."

"The first two houses that the Moors took over were old homes, right next to each other on the beachside of Highway 103. They were also two homes circled in red on the map, with parallel lines between them, which I think means a tunnel.

"And," said Ruby, sitting up and drawing nearer to Jake, "the third house where you heard Moroccan music on the night coming back from the autopsies, the old Wiggins home, that house also has a red circle around it."

"Wait. The three houses the Moors have claimed were once the homes of the smuggler? What a coincidence."

Ruby studied Jake's face as if trying to decide whether he was a smart-ass or serious. "Anyway, time for me to go to work. Ask John about it. Record him with your phone so that I can gauge his reaction. I'm a good reader of people."

"Of course," replied Jake, although he had no intention of doing any such thing.

*****

"Oh, hi, Barbara. I didn't know you knew John Ryan."

Jake was surprised to see the former Long Beach High School English teacher reading softly to the unconscious reporter, her chair drawn up tightly to the hospital bed.

"Hi, Jake. Yes, we have been seeing each other for a while. Funny expression, seeing someone, isn't it? We had seen each other around town over the years, but lately, we have seen each other in a new light."

They both looked down at John Ryan, a tube running into his mouth, making labored breathing sounds.

"So, how's he doing?"

"The doctors say he's doing well. The wound was one of those John Wayne injuries." When Jake turned a puzzled face, she added, "the bullet went through fairly clean, just like with heroes in Westerns, not causing any major damage other than a chipped bone. He should be back on his horse in a few days."

To Jake's further expression of puzzlement, she added, "Forgive me. I'm talking gibberish. Worried and nervous, I guess."

"Have the doctors put him in a coma?"

"No, they have just sedated him. At his age, his body needs lots of rest to heal. From his stories, I guess he has slept it off before, so that's what he is doing now."

Jake laughed. They agreed to keep each other up to date. Jake said he hoped she was still working on her book about her aunt and the jazz scene, placed a bouquet on the table next to John, and left.

That old coot, he thought on the way out of the hospital. Still in the hunt and still magnetic enough to have reeled in an attractive woman like Barbara.

He hoped Barbara would write her book on the aunt who left the small family town of Long Beach for the big world of jazz on the edge of its golden age. While the *Beachcomber* wouldn't publish such a book, he would like to read it.

He should give her a call of encouragement. What was her last name? It was difficult to remember. Something Eastern European sounding, challenging to pronounce, ending in -ova or -vich? Maybe Russian.

Wait! Maybe Russian? In their first meeting, she said her family had lived in Long Beach for four generations... certainly in the time of bootleggers.

And now, after seeing John Ryan around town for a decade or so, she found a sudden attraction to the old reporter? And John himself... didn't he say he had learned Russian from his first or second wife?

Was he chasing the bootlegger's silver, too? But, then, was that the story he was writing when he was shot?

Jake recalled John Ryan telling him about "killer fog" — when it envelopes a person, you can't hear anything and you can't see anything, yet you know something is out there. It's what you can't see that gets you.

A similar fog was enveloping Jake's mind — he knew something out there made sense of all these random connections, but he couldn't see what.

That something had reached out for John Ryan. Jake needed to solve the mystery, or he could be the next victim.

CHAPTER 47

"Why now, Jake?"

"Because I haven't put my pants on yet after showering?"

"Not that, silly. I mean, why all the interest in the bootlegger's treasure now after all these years? Anyone could have found it in the last 80-90 years. Why has there been this sudden interest?"

Jake felt a pang of disappointment as he slid on his blue jeans. Living with a man's lizard brain that defaults to thoughts of whoopee at the first opportunity is tough.

Ruby saw the look of disappointment flash through Jake's face. "Later, honey, later. Don't you think trying to solve this mystery is fun? Like a game? But maybe with a big payday at the end? Let's work on it together."

Jake sat down on the bed where Ruby was strolling through her phone.

"Look, I found an app that translates one language to another. We should look at those documents you found that belonged to Jane McKinney and translate them into English. Maybe it will give us clues to where the treasure is, or at least, why the sudden interest."

"Yeah, good idea," responded Jake, who thought it wasn't a good idea at all. Ruby seemed too interested in finding the treasure and had never said no to morning sex before. Were her true motives for being with Jake coming out?

"Can you bring the documents home after work, and we can have the phone translate them? I get off work at 5 p.m. I could get a bottle of wine, we'll lock the door and huddle here on the bed, all secret and safe."

Jake nodded. Bottle of wine? Locking the door? Drinking with a beautiful but dangerous woman in a locked room... Why did something that once sounded so romantic now sound so threatening?

"So you'll bring the documents home?"

"You bet. I have them hidden away, but a good idea, let's see what Jane knew," and he added, "before she was killed."

*****

"I didn't know what to do about the blood."

"Clean it up?" Jake was standing at John Ryan's desk with Bing, her head poking around his side. "I thought you would have done that yesterday when I visited the hospital to see John."

"Pffft. That's not in my job description. I think that's more like a management responsibility. Or, call in a crime scene cleaner, like on TV shows."

"The paper doesn't have the budget for that. How about you pick up the papers scattered around the floor, and I'll paper towel up the dried blood?"

"You'll be down on your knees anyway, you pick up the papers. Besides, I think I hear the phone about to ring." She turned towards her desk where indeed the phone began to ring.

Jake found a roll of paper towels in the building's bathroom, got a pan of warm water and the waste paper bin, and headed for John's desk.

Bing was still talking on the phone, taking information about a classified ad, and — it seemed to Jake — stretching out the conversation so she wouldn't be called to clean-up duty.

First, Jake repositioned the monitor on the desk, glad the bullet didn't hit it after passing through John.

He mopped up dried blood pooled on the desktop, then bent over to pick up mounds of press releases, reporter's notebooks, and handwritten scratches from John that had spilled off the desk. Reporters are not the neatest people with the best handwriting. It was always a joke in the newsroom when some zealous prosecutor subpoenaed the notes of a reporter... as if they could make sense of a reporter's unique shorthand.

A paperback book, the size of a dime-store novel, was kicked under the footwell, perhaps by an EMT working on John. On the cover was a sinister smiling gangster, smartly dressed in a suit, tie, and overcoat in the 1930s sensational pulp magazine style, smoking a cigar, silver coins running through his fingers. Behind him was an open wall safe, more silver coins spilling out. A Tommy gun leaned against the wall containing the safe.

Jake chuckled. Why did you have this, John, he wondered. The writing on the cover was not in English. Jake has seen enough Russian writing in the past few weeks to recognize the script but had no idea of the book's title.

Flipping over to the back, a shock of sudden recognition hit him. There was a small photo of Barbara — John's friend — looking decades younger but still recognizable.

"What the hell?" he muttered aloud.

"You about done, Jake? That blood is starting to smell. I may have to take a sick day."

Jake started to say, "Bing, you could help..." just as her phone rang again.

CHAPTER 48

"You've found my love child. Let me get some tea, and we'll talk."

Barbara's home, just off the main street, was easy to find. Once Bing helped Jake with her last name, they looked her up on the paper's subscription list.

"Is this you? Did you write this book?"

"Yes, and yes." She handed Jake a steaming cup.

Jake turned up a hand in puzzlement. "What's the title, and why did John Ryan have it?"

The title is *The Bootlegger's Secret Stash*. And why John had it requires a story."

"OK. I have my tea, tell me a story."

"Have you heard about Big Red, who smuggled whiskey during Prohibition?" When Jake nodded yes, she continued, "My family has been here for four generations. We came before the wave of Russians fleeing the communists. My grandmother knew Big Red — maybe knew him well — and used to tell me stories of his daring escapes from the law and the tricks he used to evade the Coast Guard.

"You have to realize, in towns like Long Beach, where the living is not easy, many people get through by skirting the law. There is a particular love for the roguish criminal. Big Red was full of personality. His stories of helping people around town were legendary — he gave out free turkeys every Thanksgiving, a godsend during the Depression — and his smuggled whiskey passed many local parched lips.

"So, about 20 years ago, I was a younger want-to-be writer, and I thought the story of Big Red, his daring escapades, his brushes with the law, his women, his mysterious disappearance, and his rumored missing treasure, would be a great first book."

"I'm hooked. Tell me more." Jake sat down his cup to free up his hands to take notes.

"I found a small publisher in Seattle who liked the idea, and away I went. I wrote the book, they printed it, and … it hit with a thud. That was about the time Amazon was killing all the small bookstores. For a small book from a small publisher to succeed, store clerks must talk it up. The small stores and the clerks were all going away.

"Listing my book on Amazon was useless, as it was buried among corporate publishers' more highly promoted books.

"Here's how bad it was. My publisher sent me 25 copies I kept on my bookshelves for 15 years. Then one May, I was having a yard sale and could not give away my book on Big Red. I could not give it away. I had a free table, and all the mismatched dishes, broken electronics, and old grubby tools flew off, but my book sat there. In the hometown of Big Red, no one was interested in history, Prohibition, or a rumrunner.

"I was picking up from the yard sale when three guys in suits walked by, eating ice cream. One of them dripped chocolate on his tie and swore in Russian. My gammy used to speak Russian to me and used to swear when she cooked, so I recognized the words.

"I took a clean wet cloth out to him and said a few words in Russian that I remembered. They were here on a trade mission — that's when our two nations were still friendly. We started talking, and one of them saw the pile of books — Russians like books — and were especially intrigued when I said the hero was a Russian smuggler. Like all Europeans, they love the lore of the West, even the reasonably modern West.

"I gave each of them a book — I was happy to reduce the pile — and they left.

"Now, this is where it gets truly bizarre. You are in

the newspaper business, right? You know, as they say, truth is stranger than fiction."

Jake nodded.

"A couple of years ago, I got a letter from a book publisher in Russia, who had obtained a copy from one of the businessmen. They wanted to translate and publish my book. They beat me up on the price — that's Russians for you — because of the translation expense and the like. I didn't care. A couple of years ago, I got a copy of the book in the mail, the book you found. And a check for 500 rubles. The book was a runaway bestseller in Russia.

"And then, I started getting a letter or two a month from Russia, from people wondering what I knew about the silver treasure. I don't know anything about the treasure. If I did, I would have found it.

"Then, I had three men from Russia drop by demanding more information. These were terrifying guys.

"Not quite a year ago, this lovely young woman came by. She, like me, was of Russian descent and also like me born and raised in America. She said an uncle in the old country had sent her a copy of my book, and she thought it was some coincidence that she and her husband were thinking of buying a newspaper in the same community where Big Red's treasure could be hidden.

"She said it could make a great story of how my book was published in Russia. But the more we talked, the more she forced the conversation to the treasure and less about me."

"That must have been Jane McKinney." Jake shook out his hand, cramped from writing fast.

"She also wanted to know if I had a large map of possible treasure spots. I printed a smaller version in the book. I said yes, loaned her the map, and have never seen it since."

"I can get you the map back. I found it in Jane's things, locked in a box at the office."

"Not important. I am sick of thinking about what I unleashed with my book. John told me he suspected the

McKinneys were killed over the treasure, and now, John has been shot.

"It was supposed to be a first book and a fun weekend read... not the opening of Pandora's box."

CHAPTER 49

"But why was John Ryan shot? He was just a newspaper reporter."

"Just a newspaper reporter? That's a little insulting." Jake and Ruby were having take-out Chinese food in their little motor court cabin. Ruby had expressed no willingness to go to the Green Hornet for bar food and didn't want to go out to a restaurant either, after being on her feet all day working in the diner.

"You know what I mean. Reporters get information from other people, they are not the original sources. Why stop him from writing a story? Did you get a copy of Barbara's book on the bootlegger? Maybe I should read it, looking for clues."

"I did. The American cover is a lot less lurid than the Russian cover. Maybe the cover is why it sold so well."

"But then, everyone else — the McKinneys, the Russians, maybe even the dead cranberry grower — has likely read the book, too. And Barbara wrote it. Do you say she has no clue about the treasure? Did she confirm there even was a treasure?"

Jake switched from chopsticks to a fork. Chopsticks took too much concentration, and he wanted to be careful with his answers to Ruby.

"She believes there is a treasure but is not sure. In her original manuscript, she had little on the treasure, mostly concentrating on the flamboyant personality of Big Red and his daring booze running. Her Seattle publisher made her play it up. Missing treasure is good for sales, although it didn't help her American sales in this case."

Looking off through a small cabin window towards

the darkening sky, Ruby tapped her front teeth with a chopstick, deep in thought. "Maybe reading the book is the wrong approach. Maybe it would be better to follow what the McKinneys were doing. Jake, I need that map Jane had and those notes she had in Russian."

"I'm sorry, I forgot them at the office. The day ran over the top of me. With John out, Pat and I have to work extra."

"We could walk down now after dinner and get them." Ruby started snapping shut the lids on the Styrofoam take-out containers.

"Whoa, you're really in a hurry. How about I bring them home tomorrow?"

"Come on, Jake. There could be several hundred thousand to be discovered." Softening her tone, she added, "And, as a newspaper guy, you like to run down stories, right?"

"You mean me, 'just a newspaper reporter?'"

*****

"Let's enlarge the map on the copier. We could pin it to the wall back at the cabin and mark off locations as we explore them."

Ruby was excitedly buzzing, holding the original map of the bootlegger's homes and secret booze landing spots Jane McKinney had borrowed from Barbara.

Red circles highlighted several squares — homes, likely — around Long Beach. Another ring was around a tiny inlet near the old ferry landing opposite Astoria. Other circles were spread over local sloughs and along Willapa Bay, the considerable body of water separating the Long Beach peninsula from the mainland.

"I bet these areas are where Big Red offloaded his liquor," said Ruby, with a finger on Willapa Bay.

Some circles had Xs through them as if marked off by Jane.

"I still can't see a 1930's gangster stashing away money

for the future. Hell, I had trouble funding my IRA while at the *Times*. Crooks are devious and shifty, but not people who think of their retirement years."

"You've known a lot of crooks, have you?"

Jake rolled his eyes. "And, if he were hiding away his loot, likely it would be as the Russian cover of Barbara's book, somewhere close where he could guard it day and night. Not buried in a mud hole along the bay somewhere."

"I think the other treasure hunters have already checked the obvious places," she said. "We should think outside the box… and I mean, outside the boxes circled in red."

She idly tapped the map with a pencil. "We need to talk with Barbara. Didn't she say her grandmother knew Big Red? Maybe if we understand what Long Beach was like during his time, we would better understand where to look."

*****

"Ah, brother Jake. It's so fine to see you again."

"It's nice to see you again, but I am shocked you are here, inside the Green Hornet. I thought Moroccans didn't drink alcohol."

Jake had ducked in to claim a familiar stool for a quick one after Ruby left for a late shift at the diner.

The big man nodded, still in a suit but not wearing his red fez today. "Yes, most do not. Moroccans are very pious people. We are more 'honorary' Moroccans. We believe in Moroccan Law, as I explained to you and your reporter, but we have not yet reached their level of piousness. Sad to say."

He saluted Jake with the wine glass and took the last swallow. "Your reporter. I am so sorry to hear he was shot. How is he?"

"He is regaining his strength every day," replied Jake.

"Do the authorities know who shot him or why?"

"They have theories, but nothing conclusive yet. One of the stories he was working on was your group and the Moorish takeover of local homes. Would you know anything about the shooting?"

"Ah, brother, the Moroccans are a peaceful people. They do not go to war against their neighbors. We try to emulate their example."

Velma slid a Mac & Jack's across the bar to Jake without him even ordering. "I also noticed the three homes your group has claimed — the two along the beach and the old Wiggins Mansion — were once owned by a notorious local gangster. And he is reputed to have stashed a treasure somewhere, perhaps in one of the homes. Have you found anything like that?"

"Ha, ha. We have not heard of a treasure from a local gangster. I am sure we would report something like that to local authorities. Although," rising off his stool, he slipped a bill out and laid it on the bar for Velma, "I would have to look further into Moroccan Law to see what it says about found treasure."

"I'm guessing you haven't always been an adherent to Moroccan Law claiming abandoned property. What did you do before this?"

Standing, the big man clasped Jake's shoulder as he passed towards the door. "Before this, I did many things. The last was a translator — English to Russian and back again. That's hard for some people to believe that a Black man like me could be an international businessman."

CHAPTER 50

"Glad you could finally make it in. The sheriff has been calling for you."

Jake reflexively glanced at the office wall clock: 8:55.

"I'm not a factory worker, Bing. I do the work when it needs to be done, whatever the time."

"Feeling grumpy today, are you?" She picked up the phone just as it rang. "Yes, he's here now."

In truth, Jake was feeling out of sorts. That second Mac & Jack's at the Green Hornet didn't help him sleep last night, nor did lying next to Ruby when she came home from the diner, wondering exactly why she was with him.

Like most guys, Jake was a fool for women, but women had also fooled him. Last night, he picked apart their relationship, looking at critical moments to see if he had interrupted them incorrectly.

Why had she approached him at the gas station? Why did she hide her face when the deputy stopped them on the highway at the scene of the RV accident, and most of all, why was she so eager to chase down the bootlegger's alleged lost treasure?

The call was from Sheriff Ramblewood, who invited him for a quick morning chat. Most of the time, being asked to the station by a cop would have set off warning bells in his brain, but today, in his mood, bring it on.

"Thanks for coming in, Jake." Sheriff Ramblewood led Jake back to her office and motioned undersheriff Snyder to follow along. Once they were all there, she closed the door.

"I take no pride in saying we have hit dead ends on the murder investigations of my uncle and the McKinneys. We also have no new clues on the shooting for your reporter, John Ryan. We are wondering if you might have some helpful ideas."

"Me?"

The two police officers stared at Jake. They were accustomed to people being nervous in their presence and blabbing away.

Jake wasn't nervous as most civilians might be, having been grilled by cops before. But he also respected their job, and his rule was to be as helpful as possible... without killing a good story. The question was: how far to go?

"Well, I did happen to see a strange, even peculiar, connection between the McKinneys and the cranberry grower," he said, deciding the story might need the help of the police.

"But, it's a long, involved, twisted story. You had better get another cup of coffee. And, you have any donuts to share?"

When Snyder returned with a paper plate of donuts and coffees, Jake launched into the story of Big Red, the booze smuggler, Barbara's book, and the legend of the lost treasure of silver dollars.

"I feel I have just sat through a Netflix movie," said the sheriff, wiping her fingers on a paper towel after consuming the last donut. "But..." she held her upturned hands out to the side in a gesture of puzzlement.

"In files Jane McKinney had locked away at the *Beachcomber*, I found a map from the 1930s, with local settings marked in red. Some of those had been crossed out. I later determined these were homes owned or used by Big Red. It was as if Jane had researched the sites but dismissed them as locations for the treasure."

"So, what does this have to do with Darrell's murder?"

Jake took a deep breath. "I found a similar map in his files at the little cranberry museum. Along with some notes in Russian."

"What were you doing in Darrell's files? That was a crime scene."

Sheriff Ramblewood shushed Snyder by making a shhh

gesture with a hand, relieving Jake from explaining how he and Ruby made a quick recon mission to the barn in the days following the murder — and were chased away by an armed person in a hoodie.

"You say both Jane McKinney and Darrell were interested in this treasure? Could be. Darrell was a local history buff, not just of cranberries. Our family has been here for generations. Family lore — although I have never heard any — could have contained nuggets about Big Red and his treasure.

"You think Russian criminals, also looking for the treasure, might have killed the McKinneys? But Darrell wasn't killed by a Russian. Your source, the female vet living in the woods, said she saw a small person bash him from behind. We have recovered the wooden cranberry scoop used, but the rain and mud destroyed any DNA evidence."

"I was told the attacker was wearing a blue hoodie. Have you found one of those?"

The sheriff glanced at Snyder before deciding to answer. "Yes, and interestingly enough, at the coach's house. But not on his side of the closet, on his wife's side. That is causing us to consider her a person of interest."

"Sheriff, when I got to John as they wheeled him out, he said, 'It's all connected,' and repeated that a time or two. I don't yet know what that means."

"Have you asked John?"

"Because of his age, they are sedating him so the bone in his shoulder can begin healing. When he woke from surgery, he waved his injured arm around, demanding a whiskey for his pain.

The sheriff laughed. "Yeah, he's a tough old bird. And we still don't know why he was shot."

"This book about Big Red. It caused quite a sensation in Russia. Maybe there is another interested party — or two — nosing around. Seen any other Russians in town lately?"

*****

Walking back to the *Beachcomber*, Jake replayed the conversation with the sheriff.

Neither she nor Snyder could recall seeing other unfamiliar Russians hanging around town. Although she told him something important: Long Beach had a large community of Russians who, 100 years ago, had fled the Communist revolution. Maybe that's why Big Red based his operations here, as he could blend in. And could find willing workers among the tight-lipped immigrant population.

Jake also wondered about the Moroccan Law people. It's just too strange to believe the three homes they had appropriated just happened to be bases for Big Red. Still, he couldn't see the Moors as murderers... opportunists, maybe, but not murderers.

He knew he had heard another Russian connection with something completely different over the past few weeks, but his mind couldn't pull up the mental file.

It would come to him... if he didn't get in the line of fire first.

CHAPTER 51

"I don't have a shift today. Let's go talk with Barbara."

Jake had detoured to the cabin he was sharing with Ruby to grab his forgotten phone, only to find her dressed and eager to explore.

"Uh, OK." Ambushed, he couldn't immediately think of an excuse not to see Barbara. "Although, she did tell me she had no clues to the fortune. I am thinking, in looking at her modest house, she would have found the fortune if she could."

"Maybe she doesn't know what she knows."

"Are you intending to hypnotize her to root out the secret clue?" Jake narrowed his eyes and leaned in, attempting to portray a mystic with the power of hypnosis.

"Follow the fingers," she played along, dancing digits before Jake's face. Then she slid her hand behind his neck, brought him closer, and kissed him slowly.

As Jake had admitted to himself earlier, he was a fool for women and no bigger fool than when a woman slipped a hand behind his neck and pulled him in for a kiss.

"I am free today," he said when the kiss ended. "Let's go see Barbara."

*****

"I put everything I knew into the book," said Barbara, pouring steaming tea into a china cup in front of Ruby.

"And, in my first draft, I didn't even make that big a deal about the fortune. I thought it was all a myth, anyway. But, the publishers thought the book would attract more sales by playing up the supposed secret treasure. That didn't go as planned until the Russians got a hold of it."

"Delicious, thank you," said Ruby after sipping her tea. "But, if there were a hidden fortune, it would make sense Big Red would have put it somewhere only he knew, but also somewhere close, where he could get it if he should have to run. By the way, what happened to Big Red?"

"You see, that is what I thought was the most interesting part of the story." Barbara straightened, leaning toward Jake and Ruby, who were sharing a sofa. "Big Red had run his operation for ten years, and then on the night Franklin Delano Roosevelt was elected president on the promise of ending Prohibition, Big Red disappeared. Gone. Poof."

"Maybe he took off to retirement, taking his fortune with him," suggested Jake.

"You haven't read the book, have you?" Barbara caught Jake out.

"Big Red owned several local assets — homes, downtown businesses, a couple of farms, and all of his smuggling boats. He left all of that, never even tried to sell them. Eventually, the county seized the properties when taxes were not paid. In today's terms, he probably walked away from a million dollars or more."

Ruby leaned in, too, eagerly picking up the idea. "I suppose the county sold off the assets. Buyers of the homes would have noticed wall safes hidden behind pictures, so I think we can rule out the homes, the same for downtown business buildings and barns on the farms. The smuggling boats could have been captured anytime by the feds, so probably, he wouldn't stash his coins there. They could have been too heavy for the light and fast skiffs."

"I will assume no new owner of one of his houses displayed sudden wealth," Jake added a cube of sugar to his teacup.

"After our first conversation, when I told you about my book, I wondered that too." Barbara pulled open a notebook sitting on the chair next to her. "I made a list of his properties and who bought them. No displays of sudden or unexpected wealth."

"Maybe we are not thinking about this correctly," suggested Ruby. "You said Big Red was a benefactor to the community — like a Robin Hood — which is one of the reasons locals didn't rat on him. Did he pay for any civic projects?"

"As I told Jake, he spread his money around during the Depression, giving turkeys to needy families at Thanksgiving, funding a soup kitchen for the hard-pressed, and paying for Little League uniforms for kids. Mostly small stuff, but visible. He did donate to constructing an Odd Fellows community hall, but that hall was torn down in the '60s to make way for an upscale motel. He knew how to get good PR."

The three went quiet. Ruby picked up one of Barbara's original books, with its cover of a grainy, black and white photo of Big Red looking dapper.

"Oh, and I almost forgot, he also paid for the Lost Russian monument at the tip of the Long Beach peninsula."

"Lost Russian? What's that?" Ruby softly ran her hand over the book cover as if looking for clues in Big Red's smile.

"Russians on the wrong side of the Communist Revolution fled their homeland. Many died, many went from wealth to poverty, and others gave up their professions to work menial jobs as immigrants in countries where they couldn't speak the language.

"The Lost Russian was a 30-foot tall statute on a small island just off the tip of the Long Beach peninsula looking longingly towards Mother Russia. You used to be able to see it when coming into Willapa Bay by boat, but trees and brush have grown up. Now, you can see it only if you know where to look... kind of like the lost Russians themselves."

"That's it! That's it!" Ruby bounced in her seat. "The Lost Russian is exactly where a sentimental Russian like Big Red would stash his silver! How do we get there?"

CHAPTER 52

"I guess now is the time to make a confession."

Jake was steering his Toyota pickup north on Highway 103 through the center of the Long Beach peninsula, past tiny towns, RV camps buried in fir trees and moss, signs for beach access, and boarded-up businesses that once were someone's life dreams.

"What confession, dear?" asked Barbara from her cramped rear seat in the small pickup.

"First of all, Jake, everything between us was honest, on my part at least. I want you to know that."

Braking for a sharp turn, Jake couldn't take his eyes from the two-lane road, but his brain — and heart — knew a "but" was coming.

"I have a rare mental condition where I count things all the time. It's called Arithmomania, and it's a compulsive disorder that I have little control over.

"I told you, Jake, that I counted cards at casinos, but that's just the tip of it. I have counted the breaths I have taken each day for as long as I can remember. I count the number of birds I see on a wire, the number of train cars going by, and the number of red cars we pass on the road. I have even counted the number of times we have kissed."

"What? No way. Where's the passion in that?"

"Oh, there's passion, plenty of passion with you. But, in the back of my brain, another number has ticked over each time we have kissed."

"Really? So, how many times have we kissed?"

"Well, my mind also likes even numbers. So remember

206

that kiss this morning, where I pulled you into me?"

Remember it? Jake's foot slipped off the gas pedal. Since his first girlfriend in high school had slowly glided her hand across the back of his neck as they kissed, he had interrupted the gesture as a sign of true love. Not consistently accurate, he had come to realize, but emotions still trumped logic.

"That was my desire to even the number... it was kiss number 600."

The people in the little pickup were quiet for a few minutes, the only sound was the tires swishing on the highway as the Toyota drove the 16 miles up the peninsula to the tip that was Leadbetter State Park.

"Is that your confession?" wondered Barbara.

"No. But it explains it." Ruby twisted in her seat to face both Jake and Barbara.

"Another part of my brain rebels at this constant counting. It seeks out disorder. It means I'm a woman of sudden, abrupt, and random changes." Looking directly at Jake, she continued, "You remember that day at the gas station?"

"Of course."

"For no reason, none; I stepped out of the car I was riding in with the man I told was my gambling assistant, walked over to you, and asked for a ride. Bang! And my life took a whole new track."

"So you weren't running away?"

"Not from him. Although I guess he took it that way, and that's why he came to Long Beach to get revenge on me — and you."

And the Hulk, thought Jake.

"Now, I want you — I need you — to believe me because the next part is a little strange."

"Uh-huh. Don't mind me, I'm a little distracted, wondering if I will ever get kiss 601."

"Don't be like that, Jake, because it doesn't make this next part any easier."

"Sorry, go ahead."

Turning back to face Barbara, Ruby said, "My family was Russian, like yours, and when I was growing up in Portland, we had this crazy uncle living with us, Uncle Rostislav, who I called Uncle Rosti. He called me his Little Ruby, although Ruby was not my given name.

"My grandparents had taken him in after he had been in a car accident during the day of FDR's election — the country went nuts that night — and he had brain damage and couldn't hold a thought long. He stayed on for decades. The Russian community looked out for one another, and he eventually babysat me while my parents were working."

"A brain-damaged uncle watched a little girl while her parents were working? That does sound odd."

"Yeah, it does. Maybe I was watching him. But that's not the odd part.

"One day, when I was a teenager, we were walking the neighborhood when we passed a garage sale. I loved garage sales and was pawing through toys when Uncle Rosti brought a book over to me. He laid the book on a table, tapped on the cover five times with his big pointer finger, then tapped his chest five times. Then he turned and walked down the street.

"That book, Barbara, that was your book on Big Red. I didn't realize it until I saw your original edition at your house today — with its original cover of an old photo of Big Red.

"I've been thinking on the ride up here that Uncle Rosti was Big Red. And his accident was the reason for his disappearance. And if there was a treasure, he had forgotten all about it."

CHAPTER 53

"So, this is Leadbetter State Park. Is that the island where the Lost Russian statute is?" asked Jake. The three stood on a small wooden dock, peering at an abrupt mound half a mile away, covered in fir trees, and surrounded by water.

"With the way high-tech money is flooding the coast, I'm surprised someone hasn't snatched up that property for a view home." Ruby nestled into Jake's side, out of the cold wind.

"That's a funny story I discovered when doing the book," Barbara said. "Big Red bought the island and then went to the county treasurer, asking to pay 100 years of property tax. Maybe he had a foretelling or was slightly crazy, like many Russians.

"Anyway, the treasurer said no, county rules forbid paying taxes ahead. Big Red insisted. He could be very persuasive. The county commissioners got involved, and since it was the depth of the Depression, someone paying 100 years of taxes on what they saw as a worthless speck in the water seemed like an excellent idea. That was 1930. They took the money, and basically, everyone forgot about it. That's a private island, still owned by Big Red or his descendants."

"So, how do we get over there?" Jake looked at the chop of the water and the wind-blowing foam flying off the top of the whitecaps.

"I'll just borrow one of these little outboards here," said Barbara. "I don't think the park service will mind, and likely, I know most of them anyway from when I taught high school."

"Er… are you sure? It looks pretty bouncy out there."

"I grew up alongside the ocean. I'm used to boating through rough water. Think of Big Red and what he'd do."

Barbara stepped into one of the small boats, pulled the cover off the outboard engine, jerked on the starter rope, and brought the machine to life.

Ruby stepped aboard. Jake hesitated. Reporting on treasure hunting over pie and coffee at the diner was more his style than actually going treasure hunting... especially if rough seas were involved.

"Get aboard, you man! Adventure awaits!" He hardly had one foot in when Barbara threw off the ropes holding the craft to the dock with one hand, turned the outboard's tiller with the other, gunned the engine, and they were off.

"Maybe slower is better," Jake shouted over the noise of the racing engine in the blowing wind.

"Nah, you got to read these waves and hit them just right, or we'll be capsized. And now, it's too far to swim for safety. You'd cramp up in this frigid water. Hold on, I'm swinging around to beach us there on that little sandy inlet."

The little boat hit the sand hard, driving ahead for a firm hold but throwing Jake over the back of Ruby.

"Gee, Jake, coming in for kiss 601?" She laughed, though, energized by the thrill of the hunt. "Let's go see this Lost Russian!"

Barbara looped a boat rope around a nearby boulder and followed Ruby uphill on a narrow path disappearing into the thick underbrush. The path hadn't been used in a long time. Jake trailed behind, slipping on moss, mud, and rocks.

Blood pounded through his body from the steep climb up the little island, and his ears still rang from the outboard, yet a tiny noise like the buzz of a mosquito caught his attention. He slapped at the air, muttering, "I hate mosquitoes!"

His foot slipped as he swung his hand at the flying insect, and he crashed down, hitting his left shin on a rock. "Ouch! Damn it!"

"Hurry up, Jake, we are almost at the top!" Ruby's voice was nearly lost in the heavy forest of fir trees. She had already disappeared up the steep hillside, and Barbara was close behind her.

Jake grabbed a limb on a small fir tree to pull himself up, but it snapped, and he fell backward on a blackberry bush. Twisting to find his footing, more blackberry thorns stabbed him. "Ouch!"

Rolling over onto all fours like a toddler, Jake clutched an exposed tree root and pulled himself upright. Looking up, both of the women were gone.

"Hey, wait up!" His voice died in the dense forest, generating no response.

Back on his feet, he cautiously climbed the hillside, occasionally kicking loose rocks that rolled downhill, crashing through the underbrush.

From below came sounds from the tumbling rocks at the base of the climb. He thought that noise must be the rock loosened by the three of them, not a creature like a bear. Although, what would a bear be doing on this tiny island?

Thoughts of a bear put a hurry in his feet, and soon he broke over the top to find Ruby and Barbara staring at a 30-foot high stone figure of a man looking westward across the Pacific Ocean.

Jake was the first to break the silence. "Good lord, that is something! I expected a little obelisk, pillar, or marker, not a massive statute."

"Big Red was a man of big gestures," said Barbara, circling the 10-foot base the stone man stood on. As interpreted by a Russian artist, the statute was highly idealized, in the classic look of Greek or Roman gods. On his head was the trademark workman's cloth Russian cap.

"I see some old beer bottles half-buried in the grass — likely from partiers — but it doesn't look like anyone has been here in years." Ruby shot a couple of photos on her phone.

Jake stood in one spot, his shin throbbing from the fall, losing his patience for the nature outing. "Do you see an X marking where the treasure is buried?"

"No," replied Ruby, "but look at his eyes."

Jake hobbled around to get a better view of the face. Poop from birds roosting on the bill of the man's cap had run down his face, and the digestive acid had etched what looked like tears.

"Oh, that is so sad," said Ruby, aiming her camera phone upward.

"No, not sad. Perfect," said Barbara. "The Lost Russian grieves for the country and the life he had to abandon."

"Let's see if a door or message is on the base." Jake ran a hand over the flat panel sides, where he could feel raised lettering. "Damn, it has eroded. I can't read anything."

"You couldn't anyway," said Barbara, bending close to the panel. "It's in Russian."

Jake knocked on a panel. "It sounds hollow. How do we open it?" adding unenthusiastically, "I guess I could go back to the pickup for tools."

He turned towards the path they had blazed through the steep forest to see a figure in a blue hoodie standing there — with a gun pointed in his direction.

"Bing?" said Jake, incredulously at the short, stout woman, her thick features obscured by the hoodie. But no, he quickly realized it wasn't Bing. And it wasn't her sisters Mary Teresa or Mary Grace.

"You must be the fourth sister. The one who was lost."

"Who I am doesn't matter. Where is the treasure? It belongs to Mother Russia and will be the salvation of the Russian people."

"Hello, Mary Faith. It's been a long time since high school," said Barbara. "We just got here. We haven't found any treasure and don't know it's here. Put the gun down. There's no need for it."

The woman in the hoodie approached the base of the statute. "Open up those panels," she ordered Jake.

"With what? I didn't bring any tools."

"I have a tool," she said, firing once at a panel.

The sudden noise of the shot, followed by a loud zing of

the ricocheting bullet, startled them all.

"Look! You cracked it!" Jake pointed at a zigzag diagonal line running through the marble panel. "Try it again."

She moved closer, placed herself just off the side of the panel, and raised the gun. When she fired, another loud blast echoed through the forest, freezing all of them — except for Ruby, who had circled the base behind Mary Faith.

With Jake's, Barbara's, and Mary Faith's attention all focused intensely on the panel and what might be revealed inside, Ruby jumped forward, grabbed Mary Faith by the shorter woman's shoulders, and shoved her hard into the statute, where she knocked her head and fell to the ground.

The gun flew loose to the ground, where the alert Barbara kicked it aside. "Get the gun, Jake!"

He quickly bent over on his throbbing leg to pick up the gun and saw blood gushing from his left arm. "What the hell!"

"Jake, what happened?" Ruby grabbed the gun from his right hand.

"I think the ricocheting bullet nicked my arm. Ow, it's starting to hurt!"

"I got this, Jake. You should sit down."

"Not until I see what is inside." He reached up and pulled away shattered marble shards

"Nothing!" said Jake and Mary Faith at the same time.

Ruby tilted her head in thought while Barbara drifted to the other side.

"Hmmm… Ruby, hand me your phone. Light from a low angle might reveal the characters in relief."

Shining the phone's flashlight app on the flat surface, Barbara bobbed her head around, trying to see the eroded writing. "Ah, yes."

"What does it say? Does it tell us where the silver is?"

"Big Red, like most Russians, could be a little cryptic. The message reads, 'Find a treasure not in what you leave behind, but where you stand.' I think it means don't grieve over the past, but find your treasure in the present."

"Yes, it could mean that," agreed Ruby, who didn't look so sure. "Anyway, Jake, I think we have the killer of the cranberry grower, and you have a great front-page story for next week. So, we did find treasure here on Big Red's island."

CHAPTER 54

Sheriff Ramblewood was waiting to take Mary Faith into custody when the four returned from the island.

"Thanks for the call, Jake. Did Mary Faith say anything?" The sheriff clicked the handcuffs tight on Mary Faith's wrists and pushed her — not so gently — into the squad car.

"She did apologize for shooting John Ryan. She said she liked his stories in the *Beachcomber*, but she was ordered to do it to keep the secret quiet of Big Red's treasure."

"Ordered? By who?"

"According to her sisters, she has long been entangled in a cult led by the Grand Mystical Adviser Rasputin. He says he is the reincarnation of the original Rasputin, who led Czar Nicholas around by the nose just before the communist revolution.

"His supreme goal is to lead a new revolution in Russia, throwing out the communists, heralding a mystic awakening among the people. They just needed Big Red's treasure to make it happen."

"I guess they don't keep up on the news. The Reds are gone in Russia, and the capitalists are in." Barbara had wetted a cloth and was wiping the drying blood from Jake's arm. The flow mainly had stopped.

"Did she also kill Darrell? But why?"

"Rasputin — the new Rasputin — was sent a copy of Barbara's book in Russian about Big Red's treasure by supporters in Russia. He realized what an opportunity the silver horde represented and asked for help. That's how the Russian gang members came to Long Beach.

"Mary Faith knew Darrell from when she was a child working the cranberry harvest. She was assigned to get his help, as he was a well-known local historian. Maybe he could help with the locations on the map in Barbara's book.

"At first, he was eager — maybe Mary Faith sweetened her offer to the single old man — but when he learned the money would go to the cult, he walked out on helping. That's when the enraged Mary Faith whacked him over the head."

"Oh, uncle Darrell...." Sheriff Ramblewood shook her head and slammed the back door to the patrol car.

"We should have a doctor look at your arm, Jake. Give me the keys, I'll drive us back." Ruby held out one palm and slid the other hand around the back of his neck, pulling him close.

"That's 601. I just wanted to get off the even number."

*****

Bandaged but no richer, Jake took solace on a bar stool at the Green Hornet.

Ruby was at the diner, Barbara had returned home to outline a sequel to her Big Red book — which she planned on reissuing on Amazon to piggyback sales on the news of today's adventure — and word had reached them on the drive home that John Ryan was waking up.

Tomorrow, Jake would write the exciting conclusion to the treasure hunt story, but tonight he checked the chalkboard for today's lineup of beers — Mystical Saviours, a Polish-style lager from Holy Mountain Brewing in Seattle, seemed fitting.

"When did beer become so bizarre, right mate?" The Australian slid onto the stool next to Jake. "I've been all around the world — Southeast Asia, Europe, South America, Greenland, and local beers with local conversations can't be beaten. But the brews these micro guys are pumping out, it's like they are trying to destroy the joy of beer drinking."

Nodding his head at Velma, he said, "I'll take a Rainier in a tinny."

Jake twisted his mouth from the first taste of the Polish lager. He sat the mug down. "Yeah, I'll take a can of Rainier, too, please."

Jake poured the light golden beer from the frosted can into a glass and asked, "I still don't know what you guys are doing here. And why did you say I made a dog's breakfast of it last week?"

"I was just having some fun with you. Dog's breakfast is a muck-up. It can also be a backhanded compliment. Nice job on last week's paper. Cheers!" Foregoing the glass, he raised the can to his mouth.

"So you're in town for...?"

"That, mate, is a story for another time. Our work here is done, though. And you and that John Ryan fella helped. I'll buy the next round, and you can tell me how you got that bloody scratch on your arm."

CHAPTER 55

When the paper came out on Wednesday with Jake's story, it was an immediate sensation.

Phones rang, people came into the office to buy extra copies, and even Bing offered praise.

"Sorry about your sister, Mary Faith," Jake offered.

"Pffft, she was always the loony loser. Not reasonable and easy to get along with like the rest of us."

Jake had written a second story for page one, tying all the loose ends together, detailing how the McKinneys' murders, the killing of the cranberry grower, the fire at the mill — caused by a falling-out of Russian thieves who had holed up at the closed mill — the tension between town people and homeless vets, the shooting of John Ryan, even the Moorish takeover of Big Red's former homes were all sparked by the hunt for liquor smuggler's lost treasure.

In a separate editorial, Jake reprised the famous FDR wartime quote, "All we have to fear is fear itself," to urge local citizens to let go of their fears and once again enjoy their neighbors and beautiful beach community.

"Every day here is a day at the beach," he wrote. "Let the tides roll on. Let's smile at each other again and love where we live."

OK, he had to admit. It was corny, and people had complicated lives, and smiling wasn't always the answer or even an answer. But readers expect their local paper to be in love with the local community. In this case, Jake was happy to oblige.

When the phone rang for him shortly after lunch, Jake expected another round of compliments.

Even better, the newspaper broker Dave Raymond was on the line. "I believe we have found a buyer."

"Great! Who?"

"Somebody right in Long Beach. It's Barbara… let's see, how do I pronounce her last name…?"

"Barbara? The local author who wrote about Big Red? She's like in her 60s."

"Ha, ha, ha. Yes. Just try finding a bright-eyed young couple in their 30s interested in owning a newspaper. You would be waiting for a long time. If not playing computer games, they are Facebooking their 500 closest friends. She says she's engaged to one of the reporters there. Not you, I assume?"

"Barbara and John Ryan are engaged? And want to buy the newspaper? How soon?"

"Right away, she says. And she plans to make the other reporter there the editor. So, you're done. Nice work keeping the place together. You have been paying attention to making a profit, right? That's what I told Barbara."

*****

"Barbara and John are going to buy the paper? That'll be worth the money for a subscription." Ruby smiled up at Jake from her stretched-out position on the bed in their small room.

"Hey, I thought I put out some pretty interesting editions."

"Oh, you did, Jake, you did. But John is a great storyteller, and Barbara has deep roots here. Once all of these crimes were solved, would you have lost interest in the ordinary news of a small-town weekly?"

"Well, I would have had you to come home to. Now, I guess we'll have to pack up and leave once the final papers on the *Beachcomber* are signed." He looked around at Ruby lying fully clothed on the bed and at their meager possessions in the small closet. "I can fit all this into the pickup, no problem."

"I don't know if I'm leaving, Jake."

"What do you mean?"

"I mean, I am not leaving. Amber has made an offer to sell me the restaurant. She wants to retire and go south to somewhere dry. I love the name Ruby's, and I'm in my uncle's hometown."

"You don't seem like a person who would be happy in one spot," suggested Jake, avoiding the bigger question.

"No, maybe not. But there's the other thing."

"Us?" That was the real question for him.

"I was thinking more about the message on the base of the Lost Russian. '...the treasure is where you are standing.' Maybe that meant living in the present, but it could have meant something different. I have begun the process of claiming that island as my inheritance. I want to stay here and see it through. And then to start digging."

"Still... Us?"

"We met on a whim. We had an action-filled romance. We kissed 649 times. Let's kiss once more and call it even and out."

Jake opened his mouth to object, but this time, his brain took over. His brain knew better than his heart. They could never go back. His suspicions of Ruby — even though ultimately wrong — had punctured their bubble, allowing doubt and distrust to enter.

So, the last kiss it was — number 650.

CHAPTER 56

"So, I'll never see the talking dolphin story?"

"Oh, it's a good one, Jake. I hope I can do it justice without you here to edit it for me." John Ryan's left arm was still in a sling, as the shoulder was taking a while to heal fully, but his barroom smile was as big as ever.

"Pat, you and your daughter have decided to stay in Long Beach and not run off to sunny Yakima?"

"I burn too easily," answered Pat, now seated at the editor's desk. "And Yakima? Too brown and dry. I'd choke over there on the dust. And now, wonders of wonders, my daughter is back to her old self. It's like she waged a two-year rebellion, won, and now we have made peace as adults."

Jake drifted over to Bing at her desk. "I meant to ask earlier, I saw you pass Levi a note when he came in to discuss his latest sci-fi idea. What was that about?"

"I offered to help him edit out all the nonsense and get his book published. I know the industry and how to make it all happen." She lowered her voice, "And frankly, I need to think of me and how I will get along if the *Beachcomber* fails." Dropping her voice even more, she added, "As it probably will.

"Oh, I have something for you." She picked up an envelope from a basket on her desk. "I wrote you a paycheck from the old owners. They weren't here to keep track of your hours, so I wrote you the same amount Miles McKinney was paying himself."

Quietly, she added, "I did mention he was a tightwad, right?"

Jake went to slide the pay envelope into his back pocket,

then realized it was already full.

"Here, I guess I won't need this," he said, laying a reporter's notebook on the editor's desk. "I'm going back to being a happy wanderer... lost somewhere down the road."

*****

A couple of miles south of Long Beach, Jake turned his pickup left onto Highway 101, a fabled highway he had yet to drive in his travels.

Soon, he was passing rural homes and rectangle ponds growing cranberries. He slowed for a turning logging truck carrying some of the smallest logs he had ever seen, then climbed a small hill with replanted tree farms on both sides.

Coming down the other side, the highway straightened, crossing through a wet area that a sign called Strawberry Slough. Somewhere off to the left was the cult home where Mary Faith had lived as an adherent of the guru Rasputin. Mary Faith was awaiting trial, but as fitting his legendary namesake, Rasputin had slipped the police net.

A big old Caddie honked twice as it swayed past Jake on the straight stretch, a large black hand waving from the driver's window. A bumper sticker on the rear proclaimed, "We're Moorish on Moroccan Law."

The day was so lovely, warm with a light overcast preventing glare from the water, that Jake had rolled down the window and rested his bandaged left arm on the frame.

Just a beautiful day... so much better than the miserable night he and Ruby had driven the Hulk into town.

"Goodbye, Jake," came a distant voice.

Who said that?

He looked past his arm into the tidal slough just in time to see a dolphin's tail fin disappearing into a splash ring.

AUTHOR'S NOTES:

While there is a town called Long Beach in Washington state, all persons, businesses, and events in this book live only in the author's imagination. Any resemblance in this story to actual persons, living or dead, is purely coincidental.

This is the second Jake Stewart novel about his adventures as an editor of a small newspaper in danger of dying. It used to be said a community needed three things to thrive: a bank to show local financial strength, a school as a belief in the future, and a newspaper to knit people together. Banks and schools seem to be doing OK, but newspapers…

The first Jake Stewart novel, *Murder in the Desert*, is available on Amazon.

Made in the USA
Las Vegas, NV
21 November 2023

81305338R00132